SPECIAL MESSAGE TO READERS

**THE ULVERSCROFT FOUNDATION
(registered UK charity number 264873)**
was established in 1972 to provide funds for research, diagnosis and treatment of eye diseases. Examples of major projects funded by the Ulverscroft Foundation are:

- The Children's Eye Unit at Moorfields Eye Hospital, London
- The Ulverscroft Children's Eye Unit at Great Ormond Street Hospital for Sick Children
- Funding research into eye diseases and treatment at the Department of Ophthalmology, University of Leicester
- The Ulverscroft Vision Research Group, Institute of Child Health
- Twin operating theatres at the Western Ophthalmic Hospital, London
- The Chair of Ophthalmology at the Royal Australian College of Ophthalmologists

You can help further the work of the Foundation by making a donation or leaving a legacy. Every contribution is gratefully received. If you would like to help support the Foundation or require further information, please contact:

**THE ULVERSCROFT FOUNDATION
The Green, Bradgate Road, Anstey
Leicester LE7 7FU, England
Tel: (0116) 236 4325
website: www.ulverscroft-foundation.org.uk**

EASY MONEY

John Cavendish is down on his luck. Released by the Pinkerton Detective Agency after suffering a terrible injury, his rent going up and his money going down, Cavendish has to take desperate measures to survive. He heads to the snowbound plains of north Nebraska where the Indian wars are raging; and where his brother Luke tells him there is easy money to be made. And when Cavendish discovers Luke has been gunned down, he is determined to find the killer.

DEREK RUTHERFORD

EASY MONEY

Complete and Unabridged

LINFORD
Leicester

First published in Great Britain in 2019 by
Robert Hale
an imprint of The Crowood Press
Wiltshire

First Linford Edition
published 2022
by arrangement with The Crowood Press
Wiltshire

Copyright © 2019 by Derek Rutherford
All rights reserved

*A catalogue record for this book is available
from the British Library.*

ISBN 978–1–4448–4859–5

Published by
Ulverscroft Limited
Anstey, Leicestershire

Printed and bound in Great Britain by
TJ Books Ltd., Padstow, Cornwall

This book is printed on acid-free paper

1

Reading, Pennsylvania, Summer 1877

The Lebanon Valley Railroad Bridge had been burning all day. As night fell, the glow in the western sky became more apparent. The breeze that had been fanning the flames for hours carried embers high into the air and brought the smell of fire to the noses of the strike-breakers.

'You easy with this?' the man marching alongside John Cavendish said.

Cavendish glanced at him. There was a glint in the man's eyes. A smile on his lips. He carried his carbine loosely on his back, the strap over one shoulder.

'They're paying us and the boss ordered me to come,' Cavendish said.

'They shouldn't have burned the bridge. That was their mistake.'

'Desperation makes men doing desperate things.'

Cavendish sensed the man looking at

him. 'You on their side?' the man said.

'I'm a soldier. I do what I'm told,' Cavendish said.

'Soldier? I don't recognize you.'

'I was generalizing. I *was* a soldier.'

'You're not from Allentown, then? Not part of the Fourth?'

'I'm a Pinkerton.'

'A Pink?'

'Uh-huh.'

'What are the Pinks doing here?'

Cavendish looked at the man again. They were marching between high buildings now. The structures blocked out the last of the light and the man's face was dark. All around them other men strode forwards, each following the person in front. It wasn't a disciplined march, not like the old days. These men had come from different places, different organizations. They had different rifles, different clothes, different attitudes.

Cavendish ignored the man's question. 'You know the cut?' he said. 'Seventh Street? Marching into it this way doesn't feel good to me.'

The strikers had chosen the Seventh Street cut as the ideal place to block the railroad. They'd set up barriers and had stopped a locomotive there. With the bridge on fire across town there were no trains moving at all.

The man said. 'I ain't from Reading. You know we don't need the Pinks. The Guard can handle this.'

'I guess someone thought otherwise.'

'Well, if you want to, you can stick close to me. We're trained for this type of thing.'

'I'll bear that in mind,' John Cavendish said.

★ ★ ★

As they entered the Seventh Street cut, walking along the railroad ties, crunching across the gravel and cinders, Cavendish found himself somewhere in the middle of the column, surrounded by National Guardsmen, militia, and tough guys employed by the Railroad. He'd lost sight of his Pinkerton colleagues way back when the officer in charge — whom Cavendish later found out was Brigadier Frank Reeder — had first set the makeshift army marching out towards Seventh Street. The high walls of the cut, chiselled vertically into the hills by hand to enable the railroad tracks to be laid flat and straight, blinkered the grey night sky and plunged everything into shadows.

But there were fires up ahead, and when the crowds of marching men started to separate — splitting either side of a stationary line of flatbeds and boxcars — Cavendish saw the silhouette of the locomotive up there. He saw men, too. Lots of men waiting for them, and in the distant light of the fires he saw they had sticks and guns.

A noise started. It rose like the grey and silver smoke from those fires, lifting and thickening, at first just jeers, then individual curses, and soon hate-filled diatribes.

'Gowen's boys!'
'Judas!'

'Come on...You...Red-hair. One on one. Now!'

'Cowards!'

'You're not brave enough, are you?'

Cavendish heard women's voices, too, shrieking down, sharp as blades.

'You're not men! None of you!'

'Oh, *you're* not starving are you? Well fed soldier boys! You don't know what it's like to starve!'

Cavendish looked up. High above them on the top edges of the cut were hundreds of people. There were fires burning behind them. Some held flaming torches. In the dancing light of those torches their faces were wild and skull-like, yellow, red and orange. They looked like devils.

Now their curses became so numerous that individual words were unintelligible. There was so much noise it was physical in its intensity, like being buffeted by a storm. Around him soldiers were lowering rifles from their shoulders, working actions, drawing deep breaths. He pulled his own six-gun free from the holster inside his thin jacket. Sweat glued his shirt to his skin. He could smell ash and smoke. The dark scent of fear and anticipation rose from the men around him.

They were deep in the cut now, either side of the blocked train. They'd stopped moving and he could hear the soldiers at the head of the column yelling at the strikers up there to move their barricades. But the soldiers may as well have been shouting into a hurricane. Their words were soaked up and thrown back at them a thousand-fold.

We should have come at them from up there, Cavendish thought. On the high ground.

Someone at the front fired a shot. Cavendish never found out if it was fired by the strikers or the strike-breakers.

Somebody closer yelled 'Let 'em have it!'

A storm of rocks and bricks, lengths of nail-studded wood, pieces of railroad iron, broken wheels, and scores of other things that weren't recognizable in the darkness, rained down on the column. The man standing next to Cavendish was hit on the temple by a rock. He swore and looked upwards, swinging his gun skywards, but then his legs weakened and he crumpled to the ground. Other men yelled. Some screamed.

Another gun went off, the explosion echoing back and forth between the sheer walls of the cut. Someone shouted, 'Hold your fire! Hold your fire!'

Now dozens of burning torches arced down from the high edges of the cut, leaving trails of sparks in the air. The men below, in an effort to avoid the flames, pushed into each other, tripping and falling. A second volley of missiles rained down on them. Hundreds of stones and pieces of metal ricocheted off the roof of the box-cars. Others rattled like gun-fire on the flatbeds.

Cavendish held his hands, one still holding his Colt 45, over his head. A rock bounced off his fingers where he held the gun and the pain scythed all the way up his arm and into his neck. Acrid smoke blew along the cut from the fires in front of the locomotive. Cavendish looked upwards between his forearms and elbows. Against the lightness of the smoke the sky was filled with so many objects it looked as if a flock of black birds was diving towards them.

There was another gunshot, this time followed by a scream so piercing that it cut through the noise like a streak of lightning briefly illuminating the darkest of nights.

'*Hold your fire!*'

But the command had come too late. It was weak and solitary in the face of all the stones and metalwork being launched at the men.

There was a volley of shots. Too many to count. Screams overlapped the echoes of the gunfire. A second volley blasted out. The soldiers around Cavendish started to shoot, too, aiming vaguely upwards at the men and women lining the cut.

Cavendish held his gun, unfired, by his side, his other arm still protecting his head, and watched the people up there pushing each other backwards, jostling to get away from the edge. One man lost his footing, his arms windmilled, and then he was falling downwards into the cut.

Something made Cavendish turn.

He saw the iron pipe a second before it hit him. Someone up there had launched it like a spear, gravity, anger, and brute strength giving it a speed that belied its weight. He saw it too late to avoid it altogether, a slim, dark shape coming down at him from a slightly less dark sky. He rocked backwards, swivelling his body away from the trajectory of the pipe. It hit him on the inside of the knee and he felt his leg snap. His body crumpled as if he'd been shot. Then the pain came and he was helpless to do anything but reach upwards with his free hand, pleading for help from anyone, trying not to scream, eyes screwed up as the agony rolled over him.

It was a full minute before anyone noticed him. By then the gunshots and the hail of stones and metal had both stopped.

It was his last day on the job for the Pinkertons.

2

Julesville, Nebraska, Winter 1877

The men rode through the snow up a slope populated by Yellow Pines. The trees grew sparsely enough that the four of them could ride in pairs, yet one of them, a kid, rode alone, two riders in front of him, one behind. The kid had his hands tied to the pommel of his saddle. The back of his jacket was dark with sweat despite the cold.

'I ain't done nothing,' he said, twisting in his saddle to look back at Caleb Stone. 'I ain't said nothing. I swear.'

Stone smiled at him.

'*Say* something,' the kid said. 'You been quiet all the way up here.'

Stone said: 'Sometimes it's best to keep your mouth shut, Lester.'

'I told you, I kept my mouth shut. I never said nothing. It's the truth.'

'We'll find out.'

'What's that mean? How you going to find out? What you going to do?'

'Just shut up, kid,' one of the other riders said.

'Damn you, Joe. Damn all of you.' The kid spat on the ground and turned to face forwards again. A moment later he said, 'I can smell smoke.'

They rode into an area where the ground was scuffed and the undergrowth flattened from animal tracks converging and crossing. A man in a blue coat hunkered down over a fire, feeding it kindling. He had a pile of snapped tree branches on the ground by his feet ready to add to the flames. He looked over his shoulder and nodded at the approaching horsemen. Another man, tall and thin with a dark beard, stood watching the riders approach. He smiled. Two missing teeth — one from the top and, right below it, one from the bottom gum — made it look as if a black stripe had been painted inside his mouth.

Tied to the trunk of the tree directly behind the fire was a young man with shoulder-length jet-black hair and the dark eyes of the Cheyenne. He wore white man's clothes and his face was bruised. There was blood clotting on his lips and nostrils.

'Cain!' the kid with his hands tied to his saddle said. 'God!' He twisted around again. 'What's going on? Please? What's going on?'

There was some snow in the small clearing, but the high branches caught most of the weather.

'How's the fire?' Caleb Stone asked the man on the ground.

'Couple more minutes, Cal.'

'Nice.' Stone looked at the riders who had ridden up with him. 'Tie this one to the tree. Then we'll have a coffee whilst the knife heats up.'

★ ★ ★

Cain, the half-Cheyenne, could hear Lester whimpering. Lester sounded like a dog that had been bitten badly in a fight and had been left outside to die. A dog that you didn't want to waste a bullet on. Lester's fingers dug into Cain's wrist, then worked their way up as far as his knots would allow, and held on to Cain's forearms. Cain could feel the sweat making Lester's cold hands slick. Lester's fingers kept twitching, kept searching for a new grip on Cain's skin, as if somehow that was going to help.

'So,' Caleb Stone said, standing up, rolling his shoulders. 'Who wants to go first?' He'd taken his coat off, despite the weather.

Cain and Lester were tied either side of the same tree. Cain was tied facing the five men who until a moment ago had been hunkered down drinking coffee. He could smell the coffee and he could smell the smoke, and it may have been imagination, but he thought he could smell the blade they had placed in the fire, smell the scorched metal, like a hot gun barrel. The men were laughing, but he knew they were uneasy. All but Caleb Stone. Stone didn't have an uneasy bone in his body. The others though, they weren't so sure. But they'd do it. They'd do whatever Stone asked of them.

'Please,' Lester said.

He was tied facing into the forest. He couldn't see what was going on. Cain knew they'd done it that way on purpose. Seeing them heating a knife was one thing. Not knowing what they were doing was worse.

'We were *going* to say something,' Lester said, his voice sounding thin and weak. 'But we didn't. I *swear*.'

'It's the truth,' Cain said. He looked at Stone. The man was big, wide shouldered. His thick beard had flecks of grey in it. His eyes were dark. It may have been the way he was standing and the darkness beneath the canopy but there were no reflections in those eyes at all. It was like looking into the eyes of a dead horse.

Stone said, 'The thing is, part of me wants to believe you. I mean, not just *wants to*. But does. But you see these boys — African Joe, there. And Arkansas Joe. And Rudy and Sam. I have a responsibility to them. It would be wrong of me just to take your word for it. You understand?'

'How can we make you believe us?' Lester said from the other side of the tree. Sobs interspersed his words.

'I figure if we ask you a few questions and you keep your story straight, then we'll believe you.'

'Please . . .'

'He's telling the truth, Mr Stone,' Cain said. One of the men over by the fire tried picking up the knife but had to snatch his hand away quickly. Another of the men laughed. *Get your riding glove*, the laughing man said. 'We were going to tell the Captain next time he came to town. That's what we were talking about when Flynn overheard us.'

'Uh-huh,' Stone said. Flynn was the agent up on the reservation.

'I thought they might look kindly on me,' Lester said.

'Who?'

'The army. The Captain.'

Stone looked over towards the fire.

'Rudy?'

'Yes, boss?'

'You deserted, too. You think the army would welcome Lester here back with open arms if he gave us all up?'

Rudy was smoking a limp cigarette. He was a lanky youth with a straggly beard, brown teeth, and hair that, like Cain's, grew all the way to his shoulders. But where Cain's hair shone with his Cheyenne heritage, Rudy's was simply greasy.

'Maybe boss. Maybe a year's hard labour instead of two or three.'

'Worth doing then?'

'*If* you want to get back in the army.'

Stone looked back at Cain. 'So Lester wanted the army to look kindly on him. You?'

'My mother is Cheyenne. My father is white. I don't want the war.'

'Some folks say my rifles will bring the war to an end more quickly.'

Cain looked at the big man. 'Maybe. Maybe not. But either way we didn't tell the Captain. We were just talking about it.'

'OK.'

'OK what?' Lester said from the other side of the tree. His voice sounded a few notes higher than its natural pitch.

'OK, let's see what we can find out,' Stone said.

★ ★ ★

Afterwards, Stone had Rudy shoot both Cain and Lester.

The smell of burnt flesh hung in the air, and it seemed to Caleb Stone that the echoes of Cain's screams were still rebounding back and forth inside his skull. He shook his head to clear the sound. He'd liked Cain. The kid was tough, and to the very end his eyes had been full of determination. Stone knew that whatever he did to Cain the kid wouldn't give in. Within reason anyway. Didn't the Indians go through rituals that were far more painful than anything he could dream up? It was a shame to shoot someone like that. But needs must. Doing it the way they had, Lester had wept and begged, prayed and cursed. He had soiled himself and he had sworn a revenge that all the men knew was never coming. Yet he had stuck to the story that he and Cain had maintained all along. And they'd never even laid a finger on him. Lester hadn't even seen what they were doing to Cain. But he could hear and he could smell and even when Cain's fingernails had drawn blood from Lester's wrists Lester had still maintained they were going to tell the Captain but hadn't actually done so.

'Cut them down,' Stone said. 'Leave them for the foxes and weasels. It'll be a long winter.'

'You happy, boss?' African Joe said. African Joe came from Virginia and assured anyone who cared to ask that he could trace his ancestry right back to Plymouth, England, and insisted his blood was as red and white as Queen Victoria's. It just happened that his skin turned dark every spring when the sun started to get warm. And it just happened that there was another Joe in the gang, too, so they'd both been given names. Arkansas Joe had stuck, but Virginia Joe had, somewhere along the line, become African Joe.

'I'm happy they didn't tell anyone,' Stone said. 'But I'm not happy they knew about us in the first place. I think I need to pay Flynn another visit.'

3

Reading, Pennsylvania, winter 1877

The red-headed nurse, Grace Nowakowski, said, 'Martha in the Post Office gave me this for you.'

She handed John Cavendish a letter. The envelope was creased and dirty, and there were fingermarks clearly visible on the edges. The letter looked as if it had travelled a long way and had been handled by many different people. But it was still sealed.

'It smells in here,' Grace said, as Cavendish turned the letter over in his hands. 'Shall I open the windows?'

'There's only one that opens. The kitchen window. The others are warped.'

She walked to his door and opened it a few inches, then she went into his tiny kitchen and he heard the scrape of wood against wood. He felt a gentle breath of fresh cold air flow into the room.

'Have you tried standing today?' she asked.

'Of course.'

She came out of the kitchen and looked at him disbelievingly. He lay on top of the bedsheets. He wore a red woollen shirt over a grey undershirt. His trousers were thin and loose with little weight to them — a hangover from when he had first hurt his knee and couldn't bear anything to touch the leg.

'Are you warm enough here?'

'I was until you opened the door and the window.'

She gave him a look that said: *Aren't you the funny one?* 'You could light the stove.'

'I'd probably burn the whole place down.'

'I'd like to see you stand. Maybe take a few steps.'

He sighed.

She said, 'I put your food in the kitchen. I clean your clothes. The least you can do is humour me.'

'What would I do without you?'

'They'd find you dead,' she said, nodding as if to reinforce the fact she mightn't be joking.

'My stick.'

In the corner of the room his walking cane rested against a three-legged table. On the table was a bottle of whiskey and a glass. There were a couple of fingers of whiskey remaining in the bottle. The wall behind the table was covered with an orange paper that was peeling away at the ceiling and beneath the window. The wallpaper was sprinkled with dark blotches of mould, some of which had caused the paper to bubble and swell, giving it the appearance of smallpox.

'*You* left it there,' she said.

He sighed again and sat up. He swung his legs over the edge of the bed.

'Keep going.'

Very gently he placed his feet flat on the bare wooden floor and pushed his hands down on the thin mattress, levering himself upright, trying to keep as much weight on his right foot as possible, grimacing when some of the weight inadvertently went down his left-hand side. He reached out for the wall, steadied himself.

Then he was upright, swaying slightly, breathing heavily, and the pain wasn't as bad as he'd anticipated. It never was. Not these days. But the anticipation of that pain was always there. The first few months had been so terrible it was as if those memories would never leave him.

'Good,' she said, smiling genuinely now. 'Very good.'

'You're a hard taskmaster.'

The truth was she had been, literally, a life-saver in the early days when the hospital had told him they'd done all they could. She had fed and washed and cared for him when he was almost as helpless as an infant with no mother.

'Your stick,' she said.

'Are they still paying you?' he asked, taking a tentative step towards the three-legged table.

'No.'

'I knew that. I asked you last time.'

'And the time before that.'

He took another step, his hands held out either side of him like a rope walker searching for balance.

'Why do you keep coming?'

'Who else is going to?'

He made it to the table. He grabbed his stick and planted it firmly on the floor, enjoying the confidence that the cane gave him.

'*I'll* pay you.'

She ignored him. They both knew he had little money.

'Come into the kitchen,' she said. 'You need to eat.'

'I will. One day.'

'What are you going to do?' She walked ahead of him, but stood aside to let him into the kitchen. There was only room for one in there, especially one with a walking stick.

'Do?' he said.

'Do.'

'I don't know.'

'Well, now you can walk again best you get to thinking.'

* * *

After Grace had left he lay on the bed and opened the letter. It was from his brother. Luke had found his way to a place named Julesville in north Nebraska. *At the edge of the plains where the land starts to rise again*, Luke had written. He always was a poet. And a dreamer. He'd spent his life crisscrossing the country and had found a particular love for the frontier, out where he could do his own thing without feeling closed in or pressurized by expectations. *You should join me. There's easy money to be had and it would be great to see you again.* John Cavendish smiled at the order of the ideas. Easy money came before seeing each other.

He dropped the letter on to the bed and stood up. It really was getting easier every time. Easier, but not easy.

It was one thing Luke talking about easy money in Julesville, but *he* needed to do something here and now in Reading. He shuffled across the room and took his coat from the back of a chair. He slipped it on, relishing the warmth. There were flurries of snow outside. Fire risk or not, he knew he was going to have to get the stove in his tiny kitchen going soon. The hot nights of summer and autumn were long gone. If it wasn't for the sweat of pain when he inadvertently put his foot down too hard, he'd have forgotten what it was like to perspire. Clutching his stick in his left hand, he edged outside.

It was time to go back to work.

4

Julesville, Nebraska, winter 1877

Flynn O'Donoghue's office was situated in an old stage-route relay station, several miles north-west of Julesville. The route had never amounted to anything, and these days the station's old stable block was piled high with sacks of horse feed, flour, biscuits, seeds, sugar, salt, and other stuff that Caleb Stone wasn't sure what it was. There were crates of tools for working the ground: knives, axes, hoes, spades and forks. Coils of rope were piled against one wall, and there were winter coats, shirts, leather belts, string, and shoes made somewhere out east and shipped to Julesville more in hope, Stone figured, than any belief that they'd be needed. There were wraps of wax paper holding candles, and matches and soap, and there were empty bottles and unused water barrels, and there were two huge iron ploughs resting up against the wall. Crates of cans without labels sat atop bags of vegetables. Only in a few of the old stalls were there horses — Flynn's beautiful piebald mare which had been a gift from the Cheyenne, a small mule that Flynn called Pig, and a chestnut Indian pony that Stone didn't recognize.

Caleb Stone led his own horse into an empty stall. He walked over to a sack hanging from a nail in the wall and pulled out several armfuls of hay, which he threw on the ground. Then he walked back outside, and around to the front of the station. He brushed snow from his shoulders and boots, and let himself in through the main door.

Flynn, red-haired and red-bearded, sat at the kitchen table sharing a bottle of whiskey with an Indian whom Stone didn't recognize.

'Mr Stone,' Flynn said, looking up. 'Always a pleasure.'

'Flynn.'

'Pull up a chair, my friend. Sit by the

stove. This is Leaping Fox. Have you two met?'

'I don't believe so.' Stone nodded at the Indian. Leaping Fox smiled back drunkenly.

Stone took a chair, twisted it around so he could rest his arms on the back. He sat down and accepted the glass of whiskey that Flynn offered him.

'You'll like this, Mr Stone,' Flynn said. 'Have a read.'

Flynn lifted the bottle of whiskey and from beneath it took a folded piece of printed paper, which he handed to Stone.

'It stops the bottle from staining my table,' Flynn said, smiling. He winked at Leaping Fox.

Stone read the notice. It was a directive from the Bureau of Indian Affairs. A reminder that a key responsibility of an agent was to actively do all they could to prevent alcohol getting into the hands of the Indians.

Stone handed the paper back to Flynn who chuckled and made a show of folding it back up and placing it beneath the bottle.

'Cigarette?' Flynn said.

'You here to buy whiskey?' Stone asked Leaping Fox.

'Yes.'

'Is this where everyone comes?'

'No.'

'Where does everyone else go?'

Leaping Fox smiled. 'They go to me, of course.'

Stone smiled. 'I need to talk to Mr Flynn alone. I hate to break up your party.'

'It's OK. I go. It's getting colder anyway.'

'I'm sorry.'

'It's OK.'

The Indian stood up. He said to Flynn, 'We go and get the bottles?'

Flynn looked at Stone. 'I'll be right back.'

★ ★ ★

When Flynn walked back into the room Stone was standing by the window with

Flynn's Remington in his hand. The gun had been leaning against the wall behind Flynn's chair. Stone tracked the Indian, whose chestnut pony was now weighed down with two large leather panniers, from the side of the building and back along his own tracks through the snow.

'What are you doing, man?' Flynn said.

Stone turned the catch on the window and pushed it open. The window squealed and a cold blast of fresh air rushed in.

'What are you doing?' Flynn repeated.

Stone sighted on the drunken Indian's back.

'Does he know?' Stone asked. His finger rested lightly on the Remington's trigger.

'Does he know what?'

'About me. About the guns. About us?'

'No. For god's sake, no. He comes here to buy his whiskey. *Your* whiskey.'

'He doesn't know about me?'

'No.'

'But he knows about the whiskey?'
'Of course. *Someone* has to know.'
'But not the guns?'
'No. Not the guns. Stone, for God's sake. He's one of you, man.'

Stone turned and looked at the agent. 'He's one of me?'

'He's half Cherokee. His father walked the Trail of Tears. His *grandfather* had a cotton business, and even had slaves.'

'What?'

'They supported *you* in the war. The Cherokee and the Grey, they were like this.' Flynn gripped his hands together in front of his heart. 'I know you like to kill. But go and find a Yankee, like you normally do.'

Stone lowered the gun and turned to face the agent.

'Shut the window,' Flynn said. 'You want us to freeze to death? Come and sit down.'

'So who does know about me, then?'

Flynn said, 'I already told you. The boys that were overheard talking about the gunrunner. Did you check them out?'

'They knew about me. But they hadn't passed word on. Though they intended to.'

'How do you know?'

'Which bit? That they hadn't said anything, or that they were going to?'

'Both.'

'We took them up into the trees, over by Pine Creek.'

'And?'

'And nothing. I got to them in time.'

Flynn said, 'Well, I don't know of any others. But it's only a matter of time, Caleb. You can't keep something like this a secret.'

'If there's someone I need to kill, tell me.'

'Like you did those kids?'

'Yeah.'

'Listen, you've had a good run, Cal. What you're doing . . . The way the Indians are killing our soldiers . . .'

'*Our* soldiers? They're Yankees.'

'You know what I mean.'

'I thought we were winning?'

'We are. Of course we are. For every

Little Big Horn there's a Red Fork. But they're still killing a lot more soldiers than anybody ever thought they would.'

'And?'

'Sooner or later it's going to come out. Probably sooner. The guns, I mean.'

'You're saying I should stop.'

Flynn poured them both another whiskey. He passed a rolled cigarette across the table to Stone, and put one between his own lips. He flicked a Lucifer into life and lit both cigarettes.'You've made good money. We both have. If you want to stay here . . .' Flynn waved his hand in the general direction of the window. Outside the snow was heavier and the afternoon was already as dark as dusk. 'Though God knows why you would. But if this place appeals, then stick to the whiskey. Hell, go out and kill a few Yankees once in a while if you must. But you wonder who else knows about you? Too many people got eyes. Especially around the railroad yard. Cal, take it from me. Unless you want to hang, it's time to stop the guns.'

Stone nodded slowly. He'd been thinking along similar lines anyway. 'I've some guns arriving in a day or two . . .'

'I know.'

'And then maybe we'll do one more run. A *big* run. Not in volume, but in *scale*. Can you ask your contact how much he'll pay?'

'For what?'

Stone said 'Gatling guns.'

5

Reading, Pennsylvania, winter 1877

Maurice Guggenheim, chief at the local Pinkerton office, said, 'It's good to see you walking again, John.'

John Cavendish bit his tongue. Aside from a few visits when he'd first been in hospital, his old agency colleagues had been noticeably absent from his life.

'There was a period when I wondered if I ever would. But Grace wouldn't let me wallow in self-pity.'

'Grace?'

'A nurse.'

Guggenheim raised his eyebrows. His whole face wobbled. It looked to Cavendish as if Guggenheim had been eating his way through the hard times that many folks were suffering.

'She's very pretty and she's an angel. Albeit a brutal one. She's also very happily married,' Cavendish said, lowering himself into the seat opposite Guggenheim, grimacing as his knee bent. 'Her husband, Alek, he's a good guy, too.'

'They're still looking after you? The hospital? The nurses?'

'Grace comes around.'

Guggenheim nodded, as if that was something to do with him, or with the agency. They'd paid for three months' worth of treatment and they'd paid Cavendish three months' worth of wages. But almost all of it was used up. He wanted to tell Guggenheim that Grace was helping him because it was what good people did. He held his tongue.

Guggenheim looked at Cavendish. 'Smoke?'

'No, thank you.'

'How about a drink then?'

He pulled open a drawer from his desk and came up with two glasses and a bottle.

'Sure. Thank you.'

Guggenheim poured the drinks.

'That was some do, wasn't it?' Guggenheim said. 'Seventh Street.'

Cavendish wanted to ask exactly which bit of the event Guggenheim had been present at. But again he refrained.

'They should never have marched us into that position. If that had been the war...'

'Still, it worked. They all went back to work.'

'Those that weren't shot.'

'It was their choice to be there.'

'It's hard being a working man with no work.'

'Uh-huh. But they had work.' Guggenheim looked at him. 'I'm guessing that's why you're here?'

'I figured you spent a long time training me, and I spent a long time learning to walk again. Maybe there's something here? Maybe there's something I can do?'

Guggenheim pursed his lips. He sighed. Then he shook his head.

'I'd like to do something, John. I really would.'

'But?'

'There's nothing. I mean, we don't

have anything here. In the office. And
... look, I saw you walk in. The stick ...
if I put you on a train right now and
something happened ... You're in no
shape, John.'

'After all I've done for the firm?'

Guggenheim sighed again.

'I wish I could, John. I really wish I
could.'

'I understand.'

'You do? I'm glad. It's good to see
you, though. Up and about, I mean. Finish your whiskey. How are you? Really, I
mean.'

★ ★ ★

The snow was starting to settle and the
sidewalks were slippery. The ice sucked
the confidence out of Cavendish's walking cane. It took a long time to get
anywhere. He was cold and damp, his
knee hurt like it had only been a few days
since that metal pipe had smashed his
bones. His wrist and hand ached from
gripping his stick too tightly.

There had been nothing at the Reading Railroad, despite the injuries he had suffered on their behalf. Nothing at the banks where their security positions were all filled. Nothing at Wells Fargo. At least the man at Reading Investigations, a new outfit just a few men strong, had bothered to write down his name and address.

He bought a bottle of whiskey, stuffed it into his coat pocket, and shuffled painfully back home, each step a worry. His money was getting to the point where very soon he wouldn't even be able to drink away his troubles. As he approached his apartment block, he saw in the swirling snow a thin man knocking on his door.

The man turned as Cavendish approached.

'John,' the man said, his face visible now, thin and pinched and red-nosed in the cold. 'I need to talk to you about your rent.'

6

Julesville, Nebraska, winter 1877

It was the railroad that turned Julesville into a thriving town. Before the spur had been laid the only people who came were weary folks heading north looking for gold, thirsty fellows heading west looking for silver, or hungry eastbound travellers looking for a break from the big sky and the great plains. They found some respite in the tents and pine cabins of the tiny town, but only enough to hold them for a day or two. Later the town had its first growing spurt when the soldiers arrived, and although the army built their fort ten miles south, the soldiers still came to Julesville to eke out what little entertainment this land could offer. The entrepreneurs brought in whiskey and food, and other goods. Business-minded folks opened hotels and saloons, and slowly the town became a viable proposition. Visitors could buy a place to sleep, a bath, a haircut, a drink, food. Their horses could be re-shod and their wagons fixed. They could find a warm body to hold.

When the railroad spur was finished, the second growing spurt occurred. Building materials arrived by train. Folks arrived by train. Food and drink and cattle and horses and more folks arrived by train. The land was cheap — even free — and though it was reputedly hard to farm, farm it they did, and the trains brought in ploughing, digging and land-breaking tools, and took away bags, boxes and crates of crops and hides and salted meat. The town expanded either side of the railroad, and extra sidings were built to hold, and load, the long rows of freight cars. They never did build a spur down to the fort, it would have cost too much, but the lack of that line gave rise to whole industry of hauliers, running carts and wagons back and forth into Julesville from the army base.

It was one of these hauliers, Reuben Scarr, whom Caleb Stone sought out the morning after he and Flynn O'Donoghue had agreed that the good times were coming to an end.

'Reuben. How are you?'

'Caleb. Cold. Yourself?'

A thickening layer of snow whitened and cleaned almost everything. Across the yard smoke bellowed from the stack of a locomotive. The heat of the boiler melted the snow that landed on the engine, and the locomotive stood out dark and huge against the whiteness like a great monster.

'It's going to get colder. You still living down by Pike Creek?'

'Uh-huh.'

'No bother from the Indians?' Stone asked.

'What do you think?'

Stone smiled. The Indians knew who the good guys were — the ones who moved the whiskey to where the Indians could buy it.

'We'll be needing a few wagons in a

week or so's time.'

'Sure. Always ready.'

'One other thing.'

'Yeah?'

Stone looked around the yard. Plenty of men were bustling about, heads down and collars up. A breeze was blowing from the north, straight down Main Street, it seemed. A girl was sheltering against the wall of the yard master's office. She had a scarf wrapped around her face. Even as he looked at her she stepped from her momentary shelter, put her head down against the snow and the cold, and turned back into town. Over by the locomotive there were several engineers with oil cans and rags doing something to the driving wheels.

'You see anybody round these parts taking more than a passing interest in what you're doing?'

Scarr shook his head.

'Not really. Some boys sometimes. Kids, you know. But not this weather.'

'No one else?'

Scarr pursed his lips.

'Maybe there has been one fellow.'

'Who?'

'Don't know him. A new feller in town. He was down in the yard a few weeks back supposedly looking for work.'

'Anything wrong with that?'

'No. But he came back a few times. He was talking to Ray — you know, Ray?'

'Uh-huh. One of yours.'

'Yes.'

'Ray doesn't know about the guns, does he?'

'No, he doesn't. I always use your boys for the guns. Anyway, this feller, he said to Ray he had an inkling of what we were doing. He wanted in.'

'What did Ray say to him?'

'Ray threw a sack of seed at the fellow and said catch.'

'And that was it?'

'Yeah. Ray said there wasn't much money in hauling seed and farmer's tools, but if he could drive a wagon he should come and see me.'

'And did he?'

'No.'

'You recognize this fellow again?'
'Sure'
'Well, if he comes back and starts asking questions you come and find me. That goes for anyone.'
'Is there something up, Cal?'
'No. And I want to keep it that way.'

★ ★ ★

Flynn O'Donoghue stood with his backside close to the stove. He drank hot sweet coffee from a tin mug and smoked a cigarette. The air outside was thick with swirling snow. It was going to be a hard winter. In more ways than one. Change was coming, and that was never good. The army was still seething about what had happened to Custer the year before. Sooner or later they were going to come down so hard on the Indians that their entire existence would be over. And when that happened he wouldn't be needed any more. But it wasn't that — he was a trader by heart, and he would find something — it was the fact that when something crumbled, when things broke down, it often revealed other things that had, until that moment, been hidden.

Maybe it was time to tidy up all the loose ends, and hide a few things a lot deeper than they were currently hidden.

It wouldn't really do to be found out as the man who had supplied all those guns to the Indians. Guns that had killed — and would yet kill — so many young white boys.

He smoked his cigarette and drank his coffee. He watched the snow settling on his windowsill and pondered as to whether or not he should kill Caleb Stone.

7

Julesville, Nebraska, winter 1877

Ella Scarr said, 'I saw him today.'

Angelina Abbot, her landlady, was standing by the stove, stirring a large iron pot filled with rabbit meat, gravy stock and vegetables. She looked over her shoulder at Ella.

'You didn't . . .'

'No. But I'm going to.'

'Ella, my dear . . .'

Ella said, 'It's why I'm here, Gina.'

Angelina took the wooden spoon from the stew and placed it on the side next to the stove. She walked across to the table where Ella sat. She pulled a chair from beneath the table and sat opposite the young woman.

'I know. I know,' Ella said. 'I should think of the consequences.'

Angelina reached out and grasped Ella's hand. 'I understand, my dear. I do.

But . . .'

'He was at the rail head.'

'Here in Julesville?'

'Uh-huh.' Something dark and angry flashed across Ella's pretty eyes. Then she smiled and her face was beautiful again. 'He didn't see me,' Ella said. 'It's a wonder I've not seen him before.'

'There are a lot of men down there.'

'He looked . . .'

'He looked what?'

'He looked happy. Good. Content, I suppose.'

'All the things you're not.'

'It just doesn't seem fair.'

'Life isn't fair, my dear. It doesn't mean you have to kill someone.'

'He needs to pay for what he did.'

'And then you'll pay for what you've done.'

'I don't care.'

'I don't believe you. Look at you. You're young, you're beautiful. You have an entire life ahead of you. Why . . . why waste it all this way?'

'It won't be a waste.'

'Yes, it will. I know you're hurting. But that won't last forever. I know. I lost my baby, too.'

'That was different.'

'I still lost my baby,' Angelina said, a hardness in her voice.

'He walked out on us. She — Charlotte — starved to death. She didn't have the strength to fight the flu.'

'I know. All I'm saying is, think on it before you do something stupid.'

'It won't be stupid.'

Angelina looked at the young woman. When Ella had first arrived in town and had told Angelina of her intent it had seemed like fantasy. How could someone so calm and matter-of-fact, so young and pretty, so . . . *normal*, insist that she was here to exact revenge on her errant husband? Ella had been — and was — so calm about it that it felt unreal. Angelina hoped, for Ella's sake, that it really was a fantasy. Something that, when push came to shove, she would realize was the province of gunslingers and Indians, soldiers and convicts, drunkards and desperadoes. Not pretty young women who had bought a gun and a ticket west.

'I've thought of nothing else,' Ella said. 'I honestly don't believe that I, or Charlotte, will rest until Reuben's dead.'

★ ★ ★

Luke Cavendish emptied his leather money bag on to the bed.

It was funny the way when you worried about money it eluded you, disappearing fast and evading any attempt to accumulate more. But when you didn't think on it, when you simply trusted that things would be OK, then the money came. That was the way it had been these last few years. A good night at faro, here, lending the right fellow twenty dollars there and getting fifty back a week later. Riding shotgun on a stage-coach and facing down some trembling kids who fancied themselves as robbers and getting richly rewarded by the company. Buying into a wagon train hauling picks and sieves and boots and gloves out to California. The money had gone up and it had come down, but as long as you didn't worry on it, as long as you put some trust out into the world, it worked out well.

On the bed were plenty of small coins, a dozen silver dollars, and a thick wedge of folded greenbacks. Plus, concealed inside one of his shirts, was a pristine new bank book with a single entry for four hundred dollars. All in all, it was more than enough to be going on with. Way more. He'd paid a month's rent already on this room, and wasn't wanting for anything. Last night he had taken that pretty Ella out for a steak meal at the Buffalo Range. She was very beautiful, and although she had some sadness in her eyes and was kind of reserved, she was well worth the romancing. Maybe he could spend a bit more on her?

But Luke was also thinking about the way that investment in the wagon train had worked out. You put money into something like that and just sat around and let the drivers take the strain. Hell, you didn't even need to be there if you didn't want to be. So long as you trusted and didn't worry on it, you got your money back five times over.

It was easy money. You just had to keep your eyes and ears open for the opportunity.

Here, his eyes and ears had led him to the railroad yard where it turned out a fellow that a few people had warned him about, a Caleb Stone, was running whiskey to the Indians. Folks said how hard and mean Stone was. Not a fellow to be messed with. A Reb who still hadn't forgiven the Yankees for burning down his ma and pa's farm. The man likes to kill people for fun. But hell, every fellow Luke had ever met had a bunch of stories like that told about him. Luke figured maybe one in a hundred was true. Anyway, so what if a fellow was tough and mean? It didn't stand to reason that you weren't open to offers. So long as fellers treated each other with respect and honesty then they could generally get along.

Yet the rumours suggested it was more than that just whiskey to the Indians.

Eyes and ears open, Luke had watched and listened, and there was talk that the whiskey was just a front. A lucrative front, but still a front.

The real trade was guns.

There were some folks who would have run a mile from that. Not through fear, though there were those, too. But because selling guns to the Indians was like setting someone up to kill your own kin.

Luke understood that. Hell, his brother John, back in Pennsylvania, had been an army man. He — Luke — would've joined up too had their ma not cried on it so much. Their pa had died through malnutrition, and John was liable to get himself killed fighting in the war, his ma said. By then it was all volunteers anyway, and so he had promised ma that he wouldn't join up. She just couldn't bear the thought of losing all of her men. So yes, he understood that putting guns into the hands of the Indians might go against the grain. But if it was happening anyway, it surely wouldn't hurt to use the opportunity to double his stake. Maybe double it a couple of times.

Luke Cavendish unfurled the wedge of greenbacks and counted them twice. Forty dollars. It wasn't enough to buy into anything. But the money he'd deposited in the bank would be. Four hundred dollars ought to be enough, though he wouldn't offer it all, of course. He'd need to figure it out a little more, need to go and talk to this Caleb Stone and work out whether it was too risky, whether or not Stone was the type to take the money and deny all knowledge.

He decided to grab a coffee downstairs in the kitchen, and then go and track down this Caleb Stone.

See if he couldn't buy into a little gun-running.

8

The Engineer was a tar-paper and pinewood shack on the edge of the railroad yard. It had no windows, and the only light came from permanently burning kerosene lamps and from what came through the door, which even in winter was left open on account of the smell from the burning lamps and the cigarettes smoked by the men who frequented the place. The men generally kept their coats on, anyway. They'd wander over from the yard, lunch bags clasped in dirty hands, and eat the food their wives had made whilst drinking the whiskey that Caleb Stone provided to One-Eyed George, who ran the place. In The Engineer, it was whiskey or nothing, and few men chose nothing.

The other thing was, even if you had no money, you could still drink there. George might have had only one eye — the other was supposedly popped out by a fellow with a knife in a bar fight in Independence, a fellow who's throat George then allegedly cut, although there was talk that George had simply walked into a tree branch one drunken night — but he could remember exactly how much any man owed him for whiskey without ever writing it down. So long as the fellow settled up on pay day George would keep extending his credit. There was a coal-burning stove in the corner of the room, and if a fellow was really cold George would boil up some coffee that usually needed two fingers of whiskey added before it was drinkable.

George, his dog, and an Indian woman who may or may not have been George's wife, lived in an old boxcar around the back of the Engineer. The boxcar still sat on its wheels, although it was no longer on a track. The fact that it was raised off the freezing ground meant that George, the dog and the woman had survived more winters than anyone could remember.

Caleb Stone placed a wooden crate on George's bar.

'Twelve bottles. That should keep you in business for another day or two.'

George blinked his one eye. The empty eye socket was hidden beneath a patch. He was bald and pale, and wore a heavy coat and a scarf.

'Much obliged. Money's in the bank. I'll get it when the rush is over.'

It was eleven in the morning, Sunday. There was no one else in The Engineer. The stove and several lamps were burning, and the room was already hazy with smoke.

'The bank?'

George blinked again. 'Some fellows wearing neckerchiefs over their faces and carrying shotguns robbed Red Mostert a few days back. Just walked into the shack where he and Doris live and took their money. They still had to pay the girls. That's only fair. Plus, the bank's paying good interest on account of so many folks are borrowing money to head up north trying to find gold. You should think about it. It's easy money.'

'And what happens if these fellows

decide to rob the bank?'

'I got my deposit book. A bank robbery ain't my problem.'

'It will be if the bank closes down.'

'I got my gun, too. I told the clerk up there. If when I come for my money it ain't there then I'll be holding him personally responsible.'

'I hope you know what you're doing.'

'Yeah. If it all works out, we might even get a proper home one of these days. You want a whiskey? On the house?'

'Sure.'

The light changed as someone paused in the doorway. Both Caleb Stone and One-Eyed George turned to see who the customer was.

'Morning gentlemen.' The newcomer was silhouetted against the grey December sky. 'I'm looking for a Mr Caleb Stone. I'm told I'll find him here.'

★ ★ ★

'Guns?' Stone said. 'Are you crazy?'

Luke Cavendish said, 'Look, I know

we've not met. If you want to call it whiskey, then let's call it whiskey. I'm just suggesting that a little more investment might enable you to bring in a few more...bottles. You must have expenses? People to pay up front.'

'I have no idea what you're talking about.'

They were sitting on the only two chairs in The Engineer, at the only table in the place. They were in the corner furthest from the door. A lamp sat on the table between the two men, painting their faces orange. A bottle of whiskey stood next to the lamp.

Luke Cavendish smiled. 'I get it. I understand. I could be anyone.'

Caleb Stone lifted his glass of whiskey. He drank the contents in one go.

'Yes, you could be.'

'How can I prove to you that I'm genuine? That I'm an investor. Nothing more.'

'You don't need to prove it to me. I don't need an investor.'

'Everybody needs investors. If they

want to grow their businesses. I've been here a while now. I heard . . .'

'What did you hear?'

'Just that maybe there was a big one coming up.'

'A big one?'

'A big deal. Maybe you need some extra investment. Maybe there are some costs involved in setting it up.'

Stone smiled coldly. He refilled his glass. He topped up Cavendish's glass, too.

'You're making a whole lot of assumptions about me.'

'I'm offering you a chance to . . .'

'Expand. I know. You've told me. The thing is, I don't need extra investment. I don't need to expand. I don't have any extra costs. Drink your whiskey. It's been good talking to you . . . What did you say your name was?'

'Luke Cavendish.'

'Drink your whiskey, Luke. Listen, George there, he was just telling me about the bank in town. They're offering good rates of return. Why not invest there?'

'There are good rates of return and there are good rates of return. Anyway, who's to say the money isn't currently in the bank?'

Stone shook his head and smiled again. He drank more whiskey.

'OK, Luke. Let's just say, for the sake of argument I was looking for investment. How much would you be prepared to invest?'

'Two hundred dollars.'

'Two hundred dollars?'

'Uh-huh.'

'You have it on you?'

'Of course not.'

'You don't trust me?'

'I don't carry it around with me.'

'But you'd hand it over when the time came? You'd trust me then?'

'We could draw up an arrangement if we had to.'

'So, you want to make this legal? You suggest that I'm running guns . . .'

'Whiskey.' Cavendish smiled.

'*Whiskey* to the Indians and you want to draw up an arrangement to invest in my operation?'

'Uh-huh. We'd both gain.'

'You have a nerve. Confidence. I'll give you that much.'

'So?'

'Where are you staying?'

Cavendish told him.

'Listen, you're crazy. You make too many assumptions. But I like you, Luke. I will be in touch.'

'You will?'

'I will.'

★ ★ ★

After Luke Cavendish had gone, George said, 'When you only have one eye your hearing gets better.'

'You heard us?'

'He's crazy. You could just take his money. Anyone could.'

'Maybe. You know Rudy?'

'Your man, Rudy? The army boy?'

'Yes.'

'If he comes in, tell him to find me. I have a job for him.'

9

Luke Cavendish was happy. It was a beautiful Monday morning. The day before, over there in the railroad yard, he had won that Stone fellow over. Of course Stone was right to be suspicious. Who wouldn't be? But the thing was, if a fellow was genuine it came across. It was in the air. And this morning that good feeling was still in the atmosphere. There was even a respite from the snow — although, looking out of his window, it still covered the ground. The sun shone down from a clear sky, and though it wasn't warm, it did make a man feel like smiling. Luke figured he'd wander over to the café and have breakfast and then see if he couldn't accidentally bump into that Ella Scarr again. The mood he was in, he'd charm her into accepting another evening out, and then who knows where it might lead?

He wetted his hair with water from

the jug and patted it into place, looked at himself in the mirror. He practised his smile a few times, did up his top button, and slipped on his coat.

Coffee and Ella. In that order.

From the boarding house it was a short walk along the main street to his favourite café — the Café Paris. The plank walks were clear of snow, but the street itself was a mosaic of horse tracks, wheel tracks and footprints, all churned into a muddy quagmire close to the edges.

He thought about Caleb Stone. Luke might have won him over, but he wasn't sure about Stone. The situation probably warranted looking into a little more deeply. Stone had a look in his eyes, a hard look, a *mocking* look at times — but there'd been something honest about him, too. Well, maybe not honest. But something honourable, was that it? He seemed like the sort of fellow who would stand by his friends and partners. Still, maybe it was a deal too far, this time.

The café entrance was off an alleyway between the hardware store and the old livery — now empty whilst some entrepreneurial types sawed up bits of it, and added other bits, all with the intent of restyling it as a hotel. The livery had moved on to the edge of town. As he stepped into the alleyway, the two-storey buildings on either side casting shadows and cutting out the pleasing sunlight, Luke saw Sheriff Johnson coming from the far end of the narrow passage. He'd never, ever spoken to the sheriff, but knew who he was — enough folks talked about the man, some with good things to say, some with less positive things. But wasn't that the way with any lawman? One's opinion would always be coloured by one's own position in respect of the law.

The sheriff was hitching his trousers up and tightening his belt. His hat was pushed back on his head and he was smiling. For a moment Luke Cavendish pondered on what was further down the alleyway? Was there an out-house down there? A bath-house? Maybe a cat-house? He found himself smiling at the thought, and at the anticipation of the coffee and toast he was about to enjoy. Behind the sheriff there was snow on the roofs of the buildings, tendrils of smoke in the air. A bird flew across the narrow band of visible blue sky.

Then Luke saw the sheriff's expression change, saw the smile vanish and alarm snap into its place. He watched as the sheriff let go of his belt buckle and fumble for the gun that was on his hip. The gun that wasn't quite positioned correctly.

Luke heard the blast of a gun behind him. He saw the sheriff's shirt burst open like a crimson flower unfurling itself in the sunshine. The sheriff was thrown backwards and Luke turned.

The fellow fired again.

He was young. Tall and lean with long, lanky hair. He had a beard that hung from his chin like long drools of dark spit.

The bullet hit Luke Cavendish in the throat and he saw no more.

10

Reading, Pennsylvania, winter 1877

Someone was knocking on Grace Nowakowski's door. She looked at Alek. He was sitting by the fire, reading the newspaper by lamplight.

'Expecting anyone?' she asked.

'No.'

She put down her knitting, rose from her chair, and wandered over to the door. It opened directly into the living room, and she'd hung a heavy curtain over the inside of the door to stop the worst of the draughts. She pulled the curtain aside and opened the door.

'John!'

John Cavendish, leaning on his stick, with the blizzard swirling behind him, smiled.

'Come in,' she said. 'Come in. I can't believe you're out in this weather. You must be crazy.'

He stamped the snow off his shoes — very lightly with his left leg — and brushed his shoulders clear of ice.

He stepped inside the room and Grace quickly shut the door and pulled the curtain.

'Good evening,' he said, nodding at Alek.

'Hello, John.' Alek still had a thick eastern European accent. 'How are you?'

'I'm almost as good as new. Thanks to your wife.'

'Come, sit down,' Grace said.

'It's lovely and warm in here,' Cavendish said.

'I bet you still haven't lit your stove,' Grace said.

She took his coat and he eased himself into an armchair facing the fire. There was a bag of wool on the floor next to the chair, all different colours. The room felt so homely it made him smile.

'A little drink?' Alek said. 'Maybe a brandy?'

'A little one, thank you. It's slippery enough out there without me being slippery, too.'

'What brings you here?' Grace asked. 'I know I'm always telling you to take exercise, but please don't tell me that's what you're doing.'

'I've come to say goodbye,' Cavendish said.

★ ★ ★

'There must be something for you here?' Grace said. 'Heading west — heading west in the middle of winter is so... *drastic.*'

'There's nothing here. I've been round and round — it's been good exercise for my leg, but that's all.'

'A man with your skills,' Alek said, shaking his head.

'I'm too slow to chase a train robber. So they tell me.'

'I'm sure we could help,' Grace said. She looked at Alek.

'Couldn't we?'

'You've done enough already. I wish I could repay you somehow.'

'You don't need to repay us anything.'

'I do. I should.'

'No,' Grace said. 'Don't talk nonsense. And why now? I mean, I know you said they're putting the rent up. But can't you wait until spring?'

'It really isn't so bad when you travel by train. And it'll be no colder there than here.' Cavendish sipped his brandy. It was good brandy and it warmed him from the inside out. With the fire warming him from the outside in he wondered if he wasn't trying to persuade himself rather than them.

'And what will you do there?' Alek asked.

'My brother is there. He's written to me and told me there is opportunity. My leg gets stronger every day. I'll be all right.'

'You have money?'

'If I go now I'll still have some left. If I hang on it'll all go on the rent. The railway . . . They've given me a ticket. I told them I got the injury saving their — business — which was the truth.'

'This summer was not good, no?' Alek said.

'No, it wasn't. I didn't blame them — the rail workers, I mean. They needed to eat, too. I just found myself on the other side. It was no different to what happened to some boys back in the war. They just found themselves on the other side. Sometimes it just happens.'

Cavendish finished his brandy. He reached out for his cane which was lying on the floor, but Grace stood up quickly and passed it to him.

'Thank you.'

'You'll come back?' she said.

'I hope so.'

'Wait,' she said. 'I have something for you.' She opened one of the doors on a small sideboard and pulled out a large paper bag. 'I was going to bring this next time I came to see you. I finished it yesterday. It's to keep you warm.'

Inside the bag was a knitted cardigan, dark blue, with a collar and large buttons up the front.

'Thank you. I don't know what to say.'

'Just be safe,' she said, and held out her arms to hug him goodbye.

11

Julesville, Nebraska, winter 1877

Caleb Stone wheeled his horse and said to the other six men, 'We go now. I know there's more as want to join too, but if the snow starts again it'll fill in his tracks and we'll lose him. Right now tracking him will be easy.'

The men nodded. They didn't want to wait either. None of them had seen the sheriff or the fellow called Luke get gunned down, but a couple of them had heard the gunshots and all of them had seen the aftermath, either down there in the alleyway or back on Main Street when the limp bodies had been carried out to a waiting cart, dripping blood on to the snow and mud.

A few people, those that had been walking by, had provided a description of the kid that had committed the killings. He was tall and thin — not lean, just thin as if he never had much to eat. He had long greasy hair and a beard. He appeared scared. The kid had lit out towards the hills on a brown horse that looked better fed than he did, and together they left tracks in the snow from the edge of town *all the way to hell*, as one of the posse said.

Stone spurred his horse's flanks and set off. The other men followed. Stone hadn't asked to be their leader, he had simply assumed the role. Most men were happy to have someone else take the lead. Not just when tracking a killer, but in life. If someone else had wanted to lead he would've challenged that man, found a reason to argue and a way to come out on top. It was easy enough to follow Rudy's tracks. Any fool could have done that. What Stone needed to ensure was that when they caught up with Rudy, it was Stone that got to him first.

★ ★ ★

Rudy was scared. It didn't feel right. It didn't feel like it was going the way that

Cal had told him it would. Cal had said that he doubted anyone would even give chase, not with Luke Cavendish being more or less a stranger in town, not with the weather being the way it was.

But that was before his first bullet had whistled straight passed Cavendish and had killed the sheriff. What the hell had the sheriff being doing down there? There had been people screaming and when he'd jumped on his horse there was even one woman, a pretty woman, had tried to drag him off his horse. He'd had to kick her on the chin. Then a fellow had taken a shot at him and the bullet had grazed his head just above his ear.

Cal had told him to make for the woodsman's hut, up on Pine Ridge. He'd told Rudy he would be up there as soon as he could with food and drink. Though for now, he'd said Rudy could just drink melted snow.

'Just lay low for a while,' Cal had said. 'No one will care about the stranger.'

But that was before the sheriff had suddenly appeared.

Damn the sheriff.

And damn Caleb. Why couldn't he do his own killing? Cal had got him to shoot those two kids they had tortured up in the woods a week before. Hell, those kids' bodies were still up there. What happened if he was up there in that hut and it was dark before Cal got there? Those kids' spirits could be roaming around. Cal could have had any of them shoot those kids — African Joe, Arkansas Joe, Sam. Any of them. Why did it always have to be him?

Damn that sheriff.

He rode with his head down against the wind and he could feel blood trickling from above his ear and down his neck. His horse was tired and although they were both sweating he sensed that she, like him, was feeling the cold. His hands were trembling. Every so often a shudder ripped through his body, though he knew that likely as not it was because of the killing rather than the temperature. He was leaving tracks in the snow that would be easy to follow so he rode through a stream for a while, the water topped with ice. Once he hit the trees it wasn't so bad, the snow on the ground was thinner and patchy. But he knew a good tracker would still be able to follow him.

Maybe he shouldn't stop? Maybe he should just keep going north. Hell, head all the way up to Dakota. There was gold up there. Perhaps he could ride through to Deadwood? He would fit in there. They liked killers in Deadwood. There was even word that Bill Hickok had been shot the year before in Deadwood, though Rudy wasn't sure if that had turned out to be true or not. But Caleb always said — and the army had said it, too — you make a plan and you stick with it, unless you need to change it. It had always sounded like nonsense to Rudy, but now it actually made some kind of sense. He and Cal had made a plan, and right now, he ought to stick with. It was only another half an hour to the woodsman's hut. He could rest up there.

Rest up, and wait for Cal.

★ ★ ★

Clouds, brown and swollen with snow, had rolled in by the time the posse entered the treeline. Flurries of snow were carried horizontally in the growing wind, and there was a heaviness to the atmosphere that suggested a whole lot more snow was coming.

'Let's get this done today,' Caleb Stone said to no one in particular. He drew his Colt 45 and rested it on his saddle. 'I don't think he'd be foolish enough to stand and fight, but keep your eyes open.'

He led the posse into the trees in single file, and with hardly a glance at the ground, he followed Rudy's trail upwards, deeper into the pines, towards the hut where he'd promised Rudy he would meet him.

★ ★ ★

It was almost dusk when Rudy saw the riders. One moment it was just trees out there, the only movement being the imaginary ghosts of the two kids he had executed a few miles away, and then suddenly there they were: six, maybe seven, riders, all appearing from the gloom, their shapes forming as if they were spirits hardening into real people.

His horse was out front of the hut. He knew he should have hidden her. But where? She was scratching around in the pine needles and the thorns trying to find food. He should have rubbed her down, too — but with what? He hadn't been prepared. None of it had gone the way it was supposed to.

He drew his gun — a Colt single action that he'd been issued with by the army. He fumbled to replace the cartridges he'd used that morning.

Where was Cal? It was meant to be Cal coming up here, not a damn posse.

His fingers were trembling so much that he dropped a round on the floor. When he stood up and looked out of the window again there was Cal, off his horse and walking towards the hut, his own gun held by his side.

'You in there?' Cal called.

Rudy looked out of the window. It was dirty and greasy and there were cobwebs that were God knows how many years old in the corners. The room was freezing cold and very dark.

'I'm here!' he cried.

'I ain't gonna shoot,' Cal said. 'But you put your hands up.'

What? Rudy couldn't figure it. What had Cal just said? *He wasn't going to shoot?* The whole thing had been Cal's idea — Cal's request. Shoot the Cavendish feller. Why would Cal be going to shoot *him?*

Then it struck him. All those other fellows there. The posse. They weren't in on it. Look at them, they had rifles lowered and aimed at the hut. One of them was cradling a coil of rope, his fingers caressing the hemp like it was a woman's hair.

It was all down to the sheriff. If that damn sheriff hadn't got in the way of a bullet then they could have stuck to the original plan. But at least Cal had figured it out. They'd raised a posse and they were going to take him back, but Cal had made sure he was in the front. Cal was telling him that they wouldn't kill him, telling him that they were going to take him back to Julesville alive. Rudy figured Cal would have a plan to get him out of jail once there.

'I got my hands up,' Rudy called. He even managed a little grin to himself. There weren't many men like Cal about.

'Tell him to come out,' one of the other riders said.

'I've got this,' Cal said quietly, and walked closer to the doorway of the hut.

'We've got him surrounded, Stone,' another man said. 'You don't need to go in.'

'I'm freezing cold, Quincey,' Cal said, his back to the riders. 'I'm not going to stand here and out-wait him. We're liable to freeze to death.'

Rudy smiled to himself. 'I've still got my hands up,' he said.

He wondered what he ought to do

with his gun. Should he throw it out of the door or put in on the ground? What would look best for Cal?

Then there was Cal, standing in the doorway, gun in his hand.

'Cal,' Rudy said. 'I didn't mean to kill the sheriff. He was —'

Caleb Stone's gun blazed three times. Rudy was still alive when he bounced off the far wall of the hut, incredulity in his eyes. The last thing he ever heard was Cal say, 'He went for his gun. The damn liar went for his gun.'

12

'Are you all right, my dear?' Angelina said. 'I mean, I can see you're not. That bruise.'

Ella said, 'He was such a lovely man.'

'The sheriff?' There was puzzlement in Angelina's voice.

'No. The one that got caught in the cross-fire. His name was Luke.'

'You knew him? They said he was a stranger.'

'I knew him.'

'They said you tried to grab the killer's leg.'

Ella said nothing.

'*That's* not the action of a killer,' Angelina said.

'Grabbing a-hold of a *real* killer.'

Ella looked at her. 'It was so cold-blooded.'

'You saw it?'

'I was walking by. I heard the first shot. I looked to my left and I saw Luke.'

'My goodness, child.'

Ella looked at Angelina. 'It was awful. How quickly a man can go from . . . He was just gone. I tried to grab the man who did it. But . . . by the time I got to Luke . . . It was horrible.'

'That's my point exactly. Your actions . . . your reactions . . . are not those of a killer.'

'No. It's different. Reuben is different.'

Angelina smiled. 'You saw a man — two men — shot dead. You tried to apprehend the killer. I think you're anything but a killer yourself.'

Ella shook her head. 'They say he's been shot dead himself. I heard it outside this evening.'

'I heard the same.'

'And that's the difference,' Ella said. 'He shot someone, and was then killed himself. I'm already dead inside. I just have to kill the man that did that to me.'

★ ★ ★

Flynn O'Donoghue didn't hear about the killings until Tuesday, the day after the murders. It was the Indian, Leaping Fox, who recounted the story. 'Caleb Stone led the posse?' Flynn said.

'Yes.'

'And he shot the boy?'

'He wasn't a boy. He was old enough to be in the army and desert from it.'

'Caleb shot him, eh? I thought he was part of Cal's little gang. His own army.'

'I believe that, too,' Leaping Fox said.

'You know he was going to shoot you? In the back.'

'Who?'

'Caleb Stone.'

'When?'

'When you met him here.'

'Why?'

'He didn't like the fact that you knew he sold whiskey to . . . well, to you.'

'He sounds crazy to me.'

'I was thinking the same. And he's getting worse.'

'Why didn't he shoot me?'

'I told him you were on the same side as him.'

Leaping Fox gave Flynn a puzzled look.

'He's a southerner,' Flynn said. 'The North burned his parents' farm in the war. His parents died soon afterwards. He likes to kill a Yankee every now and then.'

'They didn't burn our farms. They just stole them.'

'It amounts to the same thing. Stone figures that if you both have the same enemies then maybe you can be friends.'

'You think he's a friend?'

'I think you were right what you said earlier.'

'That he's crazy.'

'Yes. And what do you do with a crazy dog?'

★ ★ ★

Caleb Stone met the Quartermaster, Westlake, in a way station midway between Julesville and the fort. The station was still used to rest up and feed horses, swap teams, and sometimes drivers. Passengers could get food and maybe a little whiskey if they preferred, stretch their legs, and even sleep. The place was hot in summer and cold in winter. The food, usually pork or beef, was hard. The barrelled water was murky and dotted with insect larvae.

'I'm not sure we should keep doing this,' Westlake said. 'I swear someone's been taking a look at the inventories.'

He was a red-haired man with wire-framed oval spectacles.

His uniform was tight across his belly and his thighs, and his face was pink from the cold.

'My thoughts exactly,' Stone said.

Westlake looked relieved. 'Really?'

'Uh-huh.'

'That's good. That's really good. I mean, if they found out . . . They would hang me.'

'You've made a lot of money.'

'Yes, I have. But I'd like to stay alive to spend it.'

They were sitting on a wooden bench

in the stables out back of the station. There'd been no one in the station other than Jimbo, the manager, and there was no coach due in that day. But Stone and Westlake had got into the habit of conducting their meetings out of sight.

'Hanging's not a good way to go,' Stone said. 'You ever seen one?'

'No. And I have no desire to.'

'Depends how they do it,' Stone said. 'I've seen it done quick, and I've seen it done slow.'

'What depends on it?'

'Do it quickly and the fellow's neck is broken. That way he doesn't suffer, but his body opens up — his bodily functions, you know what I mean?'

Westlake pulled a face.

'Don't they tell you that in the army? He might be dead, but it's sure embarrassing,' Stone said. 'Do it slow, and he chokes. It's cleaner and less embarrassing, but a lot worse way to go.'

'Why are you telling me this?'

'We were talking about hanging. You want a cigarette?'

'No. I should get back. Is that it? We don't need to meet any more? We're done?'

Stone smiled. 'Almost. I figured one more shipment. Let's make it a big one. Let's make ourselves enough money that we can walk away and go and do anything the hell we want.'

Westlake stared at him. 'That's why we were talking about hanging, isn't it? You're threatening me.'

'You've got me all wrong, my friend. I've made you a lot of money and I will be offering you . . . double for this one. Maybe treble. I'm serious. How long have you got left?'

'Two years. Unless there's another war.'

Stone pulled a pouch from his pocket, opened it and took out a cigarette he had rolled earlier. 'Two years. It's nothing. I'll even put the money in the bank if you'd rather. There are good rates of interest being paid right now. You sure you don't want another cigarette?'

'No, no. Look I appreciate the

opportunity, but can't we just stop now? Leave it as it is? I've made money. You've made a lot more, I should imagine.'

Stone flicked a match into life with his thumbnail. He lit the cigarette, breathed in the smoke then let it trickle out, tilting his head and watching the smoke rise.

'It warms you up,' he said. 'You want to go inside and get a whiskey?'

'I don't want to be seen.'

'I understand.'

'So? Can we call it quits now? We don't need the money. Neither of us. Do we?'

'We don't. You're correct. But I want one more shipment.'

'How many?'

'Four.'

'Four? Four crates? That's no bigger than...'

'Four *guns*.'

'Four *guns*?'

'And enough ammunition to last, say, a day.'

Westlake looked at him. 'Exactly what guns are you talking about?'

Stone smiled, and told him.

13

Tuesday night, Sam Loude, African Joe and Arkansas Joe were drunk. They were at a table in the back of the Five Star saloon, in the dark secluded area behind the piano and beneath the stairs. One of the Five Star girls was playing the piano intermittently, and the room was cloudy with smoke. The smell of liquor and sweat and cigarettes collected at the ceiling, and the noise of the cowboys and the prospectors, the shop-keepers and the hauliers, the rail-yard workers and the professional drinkers, was loud and getting louder.

'To Rudy,' Sam said, and lifted his shot-glass.

'Rudy,' both African Joe and Arkansas Joe said, and all three men touched glasses and downed their drinks in one.

Sam lifted a bottle from the floor and refilled their glasses.

'Stupid son-of-a-bitch,' Sam said.

'Rudy?' African Joe said.

'What the hell was he doing, shooting the sheriff?'

'And the other fellow,' Arkansas Joe said. He had a leather pouch on the table and was building a cigarette.

Sam said, 'He wasn't robbing them. Leastways, he shouldn't have been. He's making good money through Cal. And there's this big one coming.'

'Shush,' Arkansas Joe said. 'You know how Cal feels . . .'

'Cal. Damn Cal and his big one.'

'You don't mean that, Sam,' African Joe said.

'You know he shot Rudy. Cal shot him. You know that, right?'

'Yeah, we heard,' Arkansas Joe said.

'Rudy drew on him,' African Joe said.

'Like hell,' Sam said. He downed his drink and refilled it. 'You think Rudy would draw on Cal?'

'There were witnesses,' Arkansas Joe said. He slipped the cigarette into his mouth and lodged it in the gap his missing teeth made. He could smoke a whole cigarette that way, without needing to remove it from his mouth. When the ash got too long he'd simply shake his head. He flicked a match into life and lit the cigarette.

'The posse was back across the clearing, is what I heard,' Sam said. 'No one saw Rudy. They've just got Cal's word, that's all.'

'Why would Cal lie about it?' African Joe said.

Sam sank some more whiskey. 'Think about it. Rudy shoots the sheriff for whatever reason and high-tails it. He's never going to get away with it, and he leaves a trail that One-Eyed George could follow. Cal's crazy about this big thing and he figures Rudy might say something once he's locked up.'

'No way,' Arkansas Joe said. 'That ain't Cal.'

'I'm telling you, he's gone crazy. He figures everyone's on to him. It's all he talks about.'

One of the bar girls walked by on the other side of the piano. She was holding a young fellow's hand and she ran the fingers of her free hand down the piano keys. The music was lost amongst the noise in the room, but Sam waited until the girl and her customer's footsteps had faded up the stairs.

'Anyway, it ain't just that,' Sam said.

Arkansas Joe puffed out smoke whilst holding the cigarette in his mouth. 'What, Sam?'

'These guns. This big thing.'

'What about it?' African Joe said.

'You happy with it?'

'What?'

'I said, are you happy with it?' Sam drank more whiskey. When he lifted the bottle from the floor he discovered it was almost empty. 'Someone else's turn to buy,' he said.

'I'll get a bottle,' African Joe said.

'You do that. And whilst you're up there, you look around, and when you get back to this table you tell me what you saw.'

African Joe fought his way to the bar and bought another bottle. He came back and put the bottle on the table and

Sam said, 'Well?'

'Well what?'

'What did you see?' Sam was starting to slur his words.

'I didn't see nothing.'

'You didn't see nothing.' Sam turned to Arkansas Joe. 'What d'you see? Or are you blind, too?'

'What's wrong with you tonight?' Arkansas Joe said.

'Cal shot Rudy is what's wrong with me. Now what do you see?'

'I see a room full of smoke.'

'And who's in that room?'

'Men, I guess.'

'No guessing about it,' Sam said. He looked at African Joe. 'Do you see men, too?'

'Yes, Sam.'

'And what kind of men are they?'

'Hell, Sam, just say what's on your mind.'

'What kind of men are they?'

'Grown men,' Arkansas Joe said.

'Drunk men,' African Joe said, holding Sam's gaze.

'They're Americans, is what they are,' Sam said.

'No they ain't.' African Joe said. 'The Polack's over there. And Grégoire the Frenchman, and . . .'

'OK, they ain't American. But what else they ain't is that they ain't Indians.'

African Joe filled their glasses from the new bottle. 'So, they ain't Indians.'

'These are our people,' Sam said. 'Americans and French and Polacks. Yeah?' He lifted his glass. 'To our people.'

African Joe and Arkansas Joe looked at each other. When Sam was in this kind of mood there was no point in arguing. They clinked glasses again.

'To our people.'

'You see,' Sam said, 'these guns that Cal wants to bring in, they're not rifles. They ain't little things. These things . . . He wants to give 'em to the Indians, and they will kill *our* people. Hundreds of 'em. Maybe thousands. You think that's right? You know Rudy was in the army? Of course you knew that. It'll be boys like Rudy riding into those guns. You think that's right? You think that's OK?'

14

The train carrying John Cavendish pulled into Julesville on Wednesday, 12 December. A porter helped carry his case off the train. He placed the case on the frozen ground. By the time Cavendish had climbed down the steps, a nickel in his hand, the porter had moved along the carriage and was helping manhandle a large trunk out of the next set of doors along.

Cavendish slipped the nickel into his coat pocket and looked around.

Smoke was blowing back from the engine. A couple of figures were shrouded inside the smoke. For a moment Cavendish was disorientated. His memory flipped backwards to that night in the summer when they had been trapped in the cut. Smoke had been blowing back alongside a train then. Shapes had been backlit against the fires that the strikers had lit. The air had been full of rock and metal. But here the air was filled with an icy blast of wind, and the smoke lifted and Cavendish was brought back to the present.

He picked up his case in his right hand, carefully gripped his cane in his left, and turned to follow the muddy path into town. Snow whitened the rooftops and drifted against the edges of buildings. Where horses and wagons and dogs and people moved, the snow had turned to brown slush. There were puddles of icy water that he was careful to avoid as he followed a few individuals away from the train. The air smelled fresher and cleaner than it did in Reading, but if he breathed too deeply the coldness burned his lungs and made his eyes water.

At the edge of the railroad yard beneath a wooden sign that rocked in the breeze on its chain, and that in a few yards time Cavendish would see simply said Station, he turned and looked out over the tracks. At the rear of the train a group of men were unloading crates from a freight wagon on to a couple of carts pulled by teams of two horses each. He could see a couple of men standing, blowing cloudy breath into cold hands, a coffin on the ground at their feet. Over on the far side of the yard smoke rose from a tiny tin chimney atop a small, soot-blackened shack. Several men hurried inside the shack carrying packages that Cavendish figured was their lunch. He wasn't sure what time it was — he had long since sold his pocket watch to pay for a few more days rent — but his rumbling belly told him it was somewhere around midday. He looked skywards. Directly above him the sun was almost hidden inside a dark sky, full of heavy cloud. Yes, midday. Time for some warm food. Time to find a room for a day or two.

Time to track down Luke and find out about this easy money.

★ ★ ★

John Cavendish placed his suitcase on the bed, undid the buckles, and opened the lid. His Colt 45, in its holster and attached to its belt, lay on top of several old shirts. He'd managed to avoid pawning or selling the gun. He had sold his shoulder holster, though. He had a full box of cartridges for the gun. Two of his shirts were a little thin for winter, but one — like the one he was wearing now — was woollen and thick. He had a pair of blue denim trousers and a pair of black trousers. He had socks and drawers. He had two books, both battered volumes of Chambers' Information for the People encyclopaedia, with a couple of bits of paper inside: his Pinkerton's contract, and his Pinkerton's termination letter. He had a couple of candles and some matches, a bar of soap wrapped in a flannel. He had a towel, a shaving kit. He had a half-empty bottle of whiskey, wrapped in the shirts. And he had the cardigan that Grace had knitted him.

'My life,' he said aloud, to the small, cold room.

But there was one more thing. Tucked inside one of the books was a photograph of Luke. Luke had paid for the picture to be taken when he had decided to head west adventuring. Something for their mother to hold on to.

There was one of John, too — or there had been, in his army uniform, the 183rd Pennsylvania Infantry. But he had no idea what had happened to that one.

He looked at his brother now. Even in the faded brown tones of the picture his brother's adventurous, mischievous eyes shone through. He'd been a handsome kid — probably still was — and in his many letters home he had often mentioned women. He appeared to have a way with them. Luke had a spirit about him, it was almost childlike at times. But it was a good spirit. He laughed a lot. He smiled. He trusted in the world and he trusted in people.

It was going to be wonderful to see him again.

★ ★ ★

John Cavendish ate hot beans, bread and fried pork, and he drank two cups of sweet black coffee in a place called Rose's Café, just down from the hotel.

Afterwards he stood on the boardwalk, warm from the food and drink. The sun had broken through a little, and although there was still sleet in the air and snow on the ground, the day was brighter. Maybe it was just his full stomach, he thought, and smiled.

He reached inside his jacket and pulled out Luke's last letter. At the top, on the right hand side, Luke had written, *Beaumont's Boarding House, Julesville, Nebraska Territory.*

'Let's go and surprise you, little brother,' Cavendish said, and turned, randomly, to the left, scouring the people walking by for someone who looked like they might know where Beaumont's Boarding House was.

15

Caleb Stone was mad. Mad with himself, and mad with some people he didn't know. So that made him madder still.

Something had been bothering him, and it hadn't been until he sat here in the smoky corner of The Engineer where he'd been a few days before with that kid, that innocent kid with the naïve and trusting eyes, that he realized what it was.

Luke Cavendish had known that Stone was planning something big.

Caleb Stone breathed in angrily, getting a lungful of smoke and kerosene fumes. He coughed and he clenched his fists.

Son-of-a-bitch.

But *who* was the son-of-a-bitch?

He'd told Flynn. That was all. Flynn was the only one. But he'd also told Flynn to ask the right people how much they'd be willing to pay. So was it Flynn?

Or was it one of the people Flynn had talked to?

Stone picked up his glass and downed the whiskey in one.

'Bring the bottle over,' he growled to George. 'And bring some more coal for the stove. It's freezing in here.'

What he should have done — and why he was mad with himself — was he should have taken the kid, the man, up into the woods like they had Cain and Lester, and worked him with a hot knife. Cavendish would have told him everything. Guaranteed. See how much trust the kid had in this world when the skin was hanging off his face. Except he hadn't done that, had he? He'd had Rudy shoot Cavendish — and that was a mess-up — and now it was too late. It was all getting out of hand, all unravelling. George brought the whiskey over, along with a bucket of coal.

'You OK, Cal?'

'I'm all right, George. Just working things through.'

'I saw 'em unloading some crates from

the train, earlier.

Reuben and Sam and the Joes. Saw someone loading the sheriff's body on there, too.'

There, that was the thing, Stone thought. If a fellow with only one eye could see what was happening, then the whole world surely could.

George folded the end of his tattered coat sleeve over his hand and opened the iron door at the bottom of the stove, releasing sparks and flames and a short burst of heat. But the icy breeze coming in through the open door snatched the warmth from the air before Stone could grab hold of it. George poured some coal into the furnace and closed the door.

'You want some pork and beans, Cal? She's making some next door.'

'No, thank you anyway, George. Tell her I said so. Tell her I said thanks.'

'You're always welcome. You're good to us. Wish there was more like you, Cal.'

* * *

'I can do two,' Westlake said. 'Not four, I can't hide four. It's not just the guns. It's the wheels, the frame, the magazines. Plus it's the cost. I can't lose that much money in the paperwork.'

Stone glared at the quartermaster.

'You can threaten me with that hanging stuff again, if you like. But it won't change anything. I can get you two. I've looked at the schedules and I wired them . . .'

'You wired who?'

'The armoury back in . . .'

'You *wired* them?'

'Don't worry. I wired a long list. Just asking what they had in the armoury. Your precious guns are hidden in a request about horses and horse feed, wagon wheels, corn, food, clothes, soap . . . You wouldn't believe how much stuff I order. So I order four, and you get two and we get two, and the numbers are changed and no one knows. And I want my money up front. Once this is done, we're done.'

'Two,' Stone said, more to himself

than to the quartermaster.

They were sitting in the stables back of the way station again. It had been a hard five miles to get there. The snow was deeper on the trails now. The afternoon was already darkening, and that snow was turning to ice. The horses would struggle on their respective rides home.

'Two. And then we're done. I know I keep saying it, but . . .'

'You giving the orders now?'

The quartermaster raised his gloved hand. 'No, but you said last time . . .'

'I know what I said. I stand by it. Two it is.'

'Then we're done? I can't keep this up.'

'Yes, then we're done.'

The quartermaster smiled.

'How soon can you get them?'

'I'll order them tomorrow. It'll take a few days at their end. Then the train . . . I guess a week or so.'

'When will you know?'

'Tomorrow they'll wire back.'

'Then let's meet back here, Friday.'
'And you'll bring my money?'
'Yes. And remember . . .'
'Remember what?'
'It's all written down,' Stone lied. 'Don't go bringing a troop of your colleagues along. If you cross me, my partner back in town has enough evidence to hang you fast and slow.'

16

Luke was dead.

The knowledge hit him harder than the metal pole that had come out of a summer night sky and smashed his leg all those months ago. Then he had fallen to the ground, screaming in agony, reaching out a helpless hand for support and assistance.

This was worse.

Too many thoughts careered around inside his head, smashing into each other, creating havoc and pain. His eyes blurred. It was as if there was a freezing wind shrieking through his ears. His heart felt like it would explode.

Luke was dead.

He stared at the lady, Mrs Beaumont. He didn't scream and he didn't fall to the ground and he didn't reach out for help. But he was aware he was gripping the head of his cane so tightly that his knuckles were white and he knew he was breathing too fast.

'He was shot dead just a few days ago,' Mrs Beaumont said. She was younger than Cavendish, maybe only thirty, but her skin was weathered, there were lines of grey in her black hair. The thick coat that she was wearing even inside her house gave her a shapeless look.

'Days?' Cavendish managed to say. His voice hoarse, his throat suddenly dry.

'Someone shot the sheriff. I'm not surprised. Your brother...You said he was your brother?'

'Yes.'

'He was in the wrong place at the wrong time. He got hit by a ricochet, I think I heard.'

John Cavendish didn't know what to say. There were colours exploding behind his eyes. He could hear the blood roaring in his ears, feel it boiling through his veins.

'Are you OK?' Mrs Beaumont asked. 'Do you need to sit down?'

He swallowed. He blinked.

'I'm . . . it's a shock.'

'I'm sure it is. Here, please. Sit down.'

'I'm fine.' If he sat down he wondered if he'd ever find the strength to rise again.

Everything was instantly different. All his plans, whatever they had actually been, were based on him and Luke running together again — figuratively, of course — like they had when they had been younger. The sensible one and the wild one. The whole a greater sum than the parts. He was alone now. Luke had been all he'd had left. Now he had nothing. All because of a ricochet.

'Can I see his room?' he asked. More for something to say than for any other reason.

'Of course you can. It's upstairs.' She looked at the cane in his hand. 'Will you be all right?'

'Yes,' he said, still fighting to clear the chaos inside his head. Yes, he'd be all right on the stairs. He wasn't sure about anything else.

'The room is empty. I haven't re-let it yet on account your brother paid for it up front. I wasn't sure what to do?' She looked over her shoulder as she climbed the stairs. 'Where are you staying?'

'The hotel by the station,' he said numbly.

'The Horizon?'

'Yes.'

'For how long?'

She reached the landing, and waited for him outside an unpainted pinewood door.

'I bought a one-way ticket.' He was breathing heavily as he made the top of the stairs. He could smell a faint flowery perfume on Mrs Beaumont.

She opened a door.

'This is your brother's room.'

He could have been back in his hotel. Plain walls with a thin coat of whitewash, a bed, a table with a jug of water standing in a china bowl, a small mirror on the wall. A wooden chair in the corner up against a small writing table. Two candles in metal dishes.

'A one-way ticket?' she said.

He stepped into the room. 'Where are

his things?'

'I didn't know what to do with them. I couldn't give them to the sheriff on account...Mr Wainlodes has them. He's the undertaker.'

'Was there much?'

'Brian — my husband — he took it all. I don't know what there was. Look, if you're paying to stay at the Horizon you should take this room. Your brother has paid for it for a month. It seems only right.'

Cavendish let his hand touch the blanket on the bed. The last place his brother slept. Would he get any sleep there?

'What do you think?' Mrs Beaumont said.

★ ★ ★

The undertaker's name was William Wainlodes. His office was along Main Street to the north, about half-a-dozen buildings south of a church that had wooden scaffolding surrounding a half-built bell tower.

Above Wainlode's door was a blue-painted proclamation: *The Undertaker.* Cavendish went inside, his cane leaving wet, circular marks on the bare floorboards, his boots leaving larger marks. The room was neat and tidy and almost as empty as his hotel room and his brother's rented room. A window, with a clean, light blue curtain strung half way up, let in subdued light. On a shelf was a photograph of a round-faced man with tufts of blond hair about the ears. He was wearing a three-piece suit. Along from the photograph was a vase of flowers, which upon closer inspection, turned out to be made of coloured paper. There was a white wooden table in the corner of the room with a chair on either side of it, and a hand bell and an unlit lamp on the table top; there was a door in the far corner of the room.

'Hello?' John Cavendish said.

There was no answer. He picked up the bell and rang it. The sound echoed loudly in the empty room.

A minute later the man from the

photograph burst into the room. He was wearing the same suit as in the picture, although now it was a little more ragged around the collar and cuffs. Over the top of the suit he wore a sand-coloured canvas apron.

'Hello,' he said, smiling. 'William Wainlodes. What can I do for you, sir?'

'My name is John Cavendish.'

'I'm please to meet you, Mr Cavendish. What can I do for you?'

'My brother is . . . was . . . Luke Cavendish.'

Wainlodes leaned forward at the waist, and twisted his head slightly, as if trying to hear better, or maybe elicit further information.

'Luke Cavendish?'

'He was shot dead, two, maybe three days ago. I'm not sure exactly.'

'Oh, goodness me. I'm so sorry. Yes, Luke Cavendish. Oh good Lord, I'm so sorry Mr Cavendish. It's John, you say?'

'John. Yes.'

'You know, I was going to write to you. About his things. There's a letter he started to you. But I couldn't find an address.'

'You have them here, his things? I assume he's buried?'

'Yes. I mean, yes and no. Mr Cavendish, John, please . . . would you like to come through to the kitchen? It's much warmer.'

'Sure.'

'Come.'

Wainlodes held open the door in the corner of the room, and Cavendish stepped through into a large kitchen with a table and six chairs, a stove burning in the corner, a window that looked out on to a snow-covered yard with a workshop the entire length of one side. The room smelled of coffee and bacon. It wasn't until he entered a warm room that Cavendish was reminded of how much the cold air made his knee ache.

'Please, sit down. Can I get you a drink? Coffee? Tea? Something stronger.'

'Coffee will be fine. Is he not buried yet?'

Wainlodes lifted a tall iron coffee pot

from the top of a bench beneath the window. He peered into the pot, nodded, and then poured some water into it from a china jug painted with bluebirds. Wainlodes placed the pot on top of the stove.

He turned to Cavendish. 'No, I'm afraid he's not buried. He was shot two days ago. It was in the morning. The ground up at the cemetery is frozen solid. We could pile brushwood on it and set a fire, that sometimes works if we let it burn long enough — and we'd do that if absolutely necessary. But with the weather as it is . . .'

'Where is he?'

Wainlodes pulled a tight smile.

'He's outside.' He paused. 'Would you like to see him?'

'I . . . I don't know.'

Cavendish thought about Luke, the Luke in the photograph, and the Luke held in his memory. The glint in Luke's eye, the cheeky smile. The way his hair flopped over his eyes when it was too long, and the way it was prone to curls when wet. His brother had been tall and lean and always full of life. Somebody, Cavendish couldn't remember who, had once said Luke rode life like other people rode a train. It was true. There were bumps and there were stops and there were tough grades to climb, but there was always a feeling of moving forward. Luke would get to wherever he was going sooner or later, and his attitude was why not do so in style? Why not do it with your feet up?

'He was . . . um . . . he was shot in the throat. I didn't clean him up or anything. I didn't know anyone was coming, begging your pardon, sir.'

'Was it quick?'

'I'd say he was dead very quickly, Mr Cavendish. The bullet severed the neck bone. He didn't suffer.'

'You say he's outside?'

'He's in the yard. In a coffin. Under canvas. It's so cold that if you want to see him he'll be . . .'

'I saw them loading a coffin on to the train, earlier.'

'The sheriff. He's going home, I believe.'

Cavendish pictured Luke's face again. The way he had been all those years ago. It was wrong to think of them as good years. They'd been hard years. The hardest. Their father had starved himself — not letting on to the rest of the family — so that they might live. And now Luke was dead. They were all dead — father, mother and brother.

'Let's leave him be,' Cavendish said.

Wainlodes nodded. 'It's wise.'

'His possessions, though.'

'Of course. One minute.'

John Cavendish looked around the kitchen, not really seeing anything. Just a few days ago he had been in another kitchen, back east, reluctant to light his stove no matter how cold, wondering on coming out here to see Luke, to bask in some of Luke's eternal warmth and optimism and joy of life. And now here he was, in a stranger's kitchen, in a snow-bound, godforsaken town, and somewhere outside in a thin pine coffin under a canvas blanket Luke slept for the last time. Cavendish wiped his eyes and let out his breath through pursed lips.

Wainlodes came back in carrying a brown suitcase, slightly smaller than the one that Cavendish had in his hotel room.

'You want to look through this now? I mean, it's yours to take. But if you have any questions. The coffee's almost ready.'

'I was told it was a ricochet.'

'Yes. So I believe.'

Cavendish shook his head. 'How can everything be changed so much by a ricochet?' He wiped his eyes again. 'Sorry, I'm not asking you. I'm thinking aloud.'

'That's OK, John. May I call you John? I understand. Sometimes it's hard to accept that the world is the way it is. It can be very cruel.'

'What do you — we — do about a funeral? You can't keep him in your yard until the thaw, surely?'

'I've built — well, the town built — a small mausoleum at the cemetery. We can hold a funeral service and then I can bury your brother there. Later, in the spring, I will move him to the ground. Would you like that? Would you like me to arrange something?'

'How much would it cost?'

'It won't be much. But as you'll find out when you look through your brother's belongings, he was a fairly rich man. Compared to most, at least.'

Cavendish stared at Wainlodes. The coffee pot was bubbling and spitting, and the bitter aroma of the beans began to fill the room. *Luke was rich?* Had he already found some of that easy money he'd written about?

'Doctor Starling wrote out a death certificate. You'll probably need that up at the bank. You'll find the doctor just two doors down.'

'I'm not following you.'

'There's a bank book. In the case. It's new. Your brother deposited some money when he came to town.' Wainlodes smiled. 'Now, about this funeral. It'll take a day to sort out. So maybe Friday? Or Saturday?'

Cavendish looked at the undertaker. Thoughts had started crashing around inside his head again. 'Friday or Saturday?'

'Yes, for the funeral.'

'Let's do it Friday,' Cavendish said. 'Let him rest in peace sooner rather than later.'

17

Flynn said, 'He's coming today.'

Leaping Fox said, 'He really is crazy coming out in this weather. It'll take him hours.'

'He wants to know how much you — not you, but you — will pay for the guns.' Flynn waved a hand to indicate he was talking about the wider Indian community.

'How do you know he is coming?'

'He comes every day or two. He wasn't here yesterday.'

They were sitting in Flynn's kitchen. The stove had been burning ceaselessly for days, and the heat had seeped into the walls and the floor and the ceiling. The windows were damp on the outside, but unlike all else outside they weren't freezing. The room was warm enough that they didn't need their coats on. A dirty skillet and two plates were on the table. They'd eaten eggs, pork slices and fried bread, washed down with coffee. Now they were drinking whiskey and smoking cigarettes.

'I've decided we need to kill him,' Flynn said. 'We talked about it, didn't we?'

The Indian looked at him.

'We need to kill him?'

'He's losing control. He shot his own man. This new idea . . .'

'The big guns.'

'It's crazy. It'll bring people — the army, the government, who knows what — down on us all.'

Leaping Fox took a long draw on his cigarette. He stared at Flynn through the smoke.

Flynn said, 'You don't agree?'

'I can disappear more easily than you. My people will hide me. They — your people — keep moving us, taking our lands, but if needs be they won't find me. But I understand why you might be worried.'

Flynn said, 'Will you help me?'
'Kill him?'

'Yes.
'Why not just shoot him when he walks through the door?'
'I need to know what he's done so far. How far he's gone.'
'Ask him. And then shoot him.'
'That easy, eh?'
'Killing is easy. Where will we get our whiskey when he's gone?'
'I'll sort that. When a man like Caleb Stone is gone, someone else always appears. It's the nature of business.
Killing is easy, huh?'
Leaping Fox nodded.
'So you'll help me?'
'You give me a signal, I'll kill him. I like killing white eyes.'
'When he arrives I'll give him a drink. Then, when I'm ready . . . I'll offer him a refill.'
Leaping Fox smiled.

★ ★ ★

Caleb Stone had bought a fur-skin coat and hat from Brewer's hardware store on Main Street. Rye Brewer told Stone the coat had belonged to a mountain man who came back east after supposedly making a small fortune. Brewer said the fortune turned out to be small enough that the man had had to sell the coat in order to fund the rest of his journey home. 'I then sold it to a fellow who was heading up to the Black Hills, but a horse kicked him in the shin before he left. Shattered the bone and he had to return east, too.'

'The coat's full of good luck, is what you're telling me,' Stone had laughed.

'If you believe in such things and it's put you off, then I can sell you a nice new one from Chicago instead,' Brewer said. 'Ain't so warm, costs twice as much, and won't last half as long. But nobody's died in it.'

'Someone's died in this one?' Stone said.

Brewer had laughed and winked. 'Not yet, Cal,' he'd joked. 'Not yet.'

Stone bought an extra blanket for his horse, too.

Now, as he approached Flynn's Agency office, he was glad of the warmth the coat and hat gave him, and he felt better knowing that he could lay the blanket over his horse whilst he sat inside Flynn's kitchen by the stove.

There was smoke coming from Flynn's chimney, and one of the windows facing the trail was lit up from the inside by a flickering orange candle. Stone wiped snow from his eyes with gloved hands, and shuddered involuntarily deep inside the furs.

It was a godforsaken country in winter, for sure. After this last shipment was done and he'd been paid he was going to head south. Somewhere dry. Hell, maybe even Mexico. Somewhere where there was sunshine even in winter.

He felt his horse slip a little on the ice. She moved forwards gingerly.

'It's OK,' he said, and placed a glove on her neck. 'Almost there.'

★ ★ ★

Leaping Fox sat at the table with his back to the door, smoking a cigarette and with his hand wrapped around a glass of whiskey. He had a Colt Single Action revolver on the table next to the whiskey. A rush of cold air swept through the building as Caleb Stone opened and closed the outside door. Even after Stone closed the door that cold air filled the kitchen and caressed Leaping Fox's neck and made him shiver. It was as if the freezing air was bigger and stronger than all that warmth Flynn had built up in the kitchen.

'In here,' Flynn called, as if he'd be anywhere else but the kitchen.

Stone walked in, looking like a wide-shouldered giant in his fur coat and a fur hat. The fur had captured the weather and the coldness enveloped Stone like a spirit that Leaping Fox couldn't see, but could feel. He shivered again.

'You live here these days?' Stone said.

'It's warmer than my lodge,' Leaping Fox said.

'Sit here,' Flynn said, pulling out the chair nearest the stove. 'You didn't have to come.'

'Yes I did.'

Stone sat down by the stove and pulled his gloves off. He removed his hat, blinked and shook his head to clear snow from his eyelashes.

'This'll warm you,' Flynn said, and put a glass of whiskey on the table in front of Stone.

Stone downed the whiskey in a single go. He closed his eyes as the alcohol warmed his insides, and whilst Stone's eyes were closed Flynn shook his head at Leaping Fox. Not yet.

'Figure you need a refill already,' Flynn said, and poured more whiskey into Stone's glass.

Stone untied the loops on the front of his coat and let the thick fur flop open. He looked at Flynn and then at Leaping Fox. He looked back at Flynn and tilted his head slightly, an unspoken question in the air.

'It's OK,' Flynn said.

'Not with him here, it isn't.'

'He's OK.'

'He's the whiskey man. The whiskey man that drinks his own profits.'

'I'm just warming myself, the same as you,' Leaping Fox said.

'You can trust him,' Flynn said.

Stone looked from one to the other again. 'You told me he knows about the whiskey and that was all.'

'That was all. But he's the only one will come up here this weather.'

Stone glared at Leaping Fox. 'So now he knows what?'

'Now he knows there's a proposition in the air.'

'A proposition, is that what you call it? What you're saying is that someone else knows my business now. Another person?'

'Cal, you have to trust some people. He's the go-between.'

Stone took a drink of whiskey. He sighed.

'I saw our man from the fort, yesterday.' He looked at Flynn, then at Leaping

Fox. 'He can get the guns.'

'Good,' Flynn said.

'But, he can only get two.'

'Two,' Leaping Fox said, a hint of disappointment in his voice.

'Yes, two. That's better than none, wouldn't you say? Question is, how much are you going to pay? You want me to give my man the go-ahead, you have to be prepared to pay.'

'You've not . . . *ordered* them yet, then?' Flynn asked.

Stone lifted his glass and drank half of his remaining whiskey.

'Oh, they're on their way. Question is, are they going to go to the fort or the reservation? Two of 'em, anyway.'

'We'll pay,' Leaping Fox said.

'How much?'

'There will be ammunition?'

'I thought he said you *knew?* Of course there'll be ammunition. I always supply ammunition. There'll be more rounds than you know what to do with. You get the wheels and the frame and the guns. Everything.'

'For two, we'll pay you a thousand dollars,' Leaping Fox said. He sipped whiskey and then he raised his cigarette to his lips. He smiled.

'A thousand dollars?'

'Yes. For two.'

Stone nodded. Then he grunted happily. 'Wish I could've got you all four, then.' He nodded again, he smiled, and then he spat on his hand and held it out towards Leaping Fox.

Leaping Fox spat lightly on his own hand.

He leant forwards and shook hands with Stone.

'A thousand dollars,' Stone said. He lifted his glass and finished his whiskey in a single swallow. 'I like this man.'

'Refill?' Flynn asked.

Caleb Stone leaned back in the seat as Flynn stepped to the side of him, whiskey bottle in his hand. A thousand easy dollars. After he'd paid everyone he'd clear half that himself. Maybe more. The guns themselves would be paid for by the US Army. That was the beauty of it all.

It was a shame that Westlake couldn't have figured out a way to divert all four guns, but heck, five hundred dollars, along with what he'd already amassed, was more than enough to get him down south once again.

Flynn was filling his glass again, standing awkwardly as if scared to get too close. What was that all about?

Then Stone saw the Indian picking up the gun that had been lying on the table. The Indian's face was expressionless, his eyes cold and dark.

'What the hell,' Stone said, kicking his feet against the wooden floor, trying to push his chair out from under the table to make some space.

The Indian was raising the gun now.

The damn fur coat was too big, too bulky. His own gun was under there somewhere, underneath the fur coat and the jacket beneath it, and both coat and jacket were all caught up beneath the table.

He heard the ratcheting of the hammer as the Indian squeezed the trigger.

He tried to stand but his feet felt tangled.

The gunshot exploded in the hot kitchen. Stone saw the flames and he felt the pressure on his ear-drums and he smelled the gunpowder and cordite.

He heard the scream.

And he watched Flynn fly backwards, dropping the whiskey bottle, smashing into the stove, sliding to the ground, eyes wide open in fear and surprise, as the wound in his chest poured blood and life out into the warm room.

18

Mrs Beaumont had a new dress on. It was floor length, and brown and white stripes ran the length of it. There was lace at the neck and at the wrists, and a soft dark red leather belt was tied around her waist.

'You look fine this morning, Mrs Beaumont,' John Cavendish said.

'Thank you. Please call me Myra, though. Mrs Beaumont sounds so formal.'

'You look fine this morning, Myra.'

Was she blushing a little, he wondered.

'Can I make you a drink?' she asked.

'No, thank you. I'm going to take a wander down to the alleyway where . . .' He let the words hang.

'Where your brother was shot?'

'Yes. I want to see for myself. Maybe ask a few questions.'

'Questions?'

'Yes. I just need to understand what

happened. To picture it.'

'Does that not . . . make it real? Make it worse?'

'Yes and yes,' Cavendish said. 'But it's real enough anyway. I've just been looking through his things. He'd written some stuff down. I don't know. I guess I need to persuade myself that a ricochet, that chance, really is to blame.'

'It really was terrible luck,' she said. He leaned on his cane and wondered why she suddenly looked so guilty in her new dress.

★ ★ ★

Luke's second letter from Julesville had been unfinished. Luke sounded somewhat less excited in it than he had in the one that had made it all the way to Pennsylvania, but he still talked about seeing John again.

> Easy money? I'm not sure now. I've sounded them out and even made an offer, but they're playing

dumb. Maybe it's too risky, anyway. I have a feeling they'd take my money and deny all knowledge. Some things — some people — live just too far the other side of the law, I guess.

But you should still come, John. Maybe wait until spring? Depends what you're doing for a living, I suppose. There's a real pretty girl here, Ella. I reckon by spring she might have fallen for my charms. And by spring I will have found a way to make money here. If I haven't, then maybe we could ride up to the Black Hills together?

Anyway . . .

And that's where it finished: *Anyway* — a sentence left hanging. A letter left unfinished and never sent. And what were the chances of him ever having seen it if he hadn't come to Julesville?

John Cavendish didn't believe in fate. Although some nights, when he had been cold and hungry, when his leg had been hurting and he had been unable to sleep for thinking about the fact that he had been in a column of strike-breakers when he had received the injury, life did seem rather fateful. He could just imagine his father's face had he known what his boy had been doing. John Cavendish senior had worked in a mill until he'd had a hand crushed when his eldest son was no more than eight or nine. They lived in three tiny rooms in a falling down brick building deep in the maze known as White City. Their mother worked at a bakery and did a little sewing. Both of them — ma and pa — doing whatever they could to make things less hard. But it was hard. It was hot in the summer and cold in the winter, and sometimes they had no shoes and sometimes they had no food.

His father would have been up there, high on the edges of the Seventh Street cut, fighting for their chance to live a little, rather than die slowly. *He* wouldn't have been down in the line of strike-breakers. John knew he would have been unable to make his father understand why *he* had been where he was. He wouldn't have had the words to describe, in a way that John senior would have grasped, that it was precisely *because* of those hard times, it was the fear of losing that job, the fear of starving to death the way he had seen his father do. *That's* why he had done what the Pinks had asked him to do — and he wasn't proud of it.

But hadn't that last job been, ultimately, what had brought him here?

Now, still pondering on fate, he found himself wondering if there was a reason for it. And if so, surely it was not to discover that a random ricochet in an alleyway had killed his brother. Not when Luke had written *I've sounded them out and even made an offer, but they're playing dumb. Maybe it's too risky, anyway. I have a feeling they'd take my money and deny all knowledge. Some things — some people — are just too far the other side of the law, I guess.*

No, fate or not, there had to be more to it.

★ ★ ★

Wainlodes had been correct about the money. A bank book, new and uncreased, drawn on the bank right here in Julesville, showed a deposit of four hundred dollars.

Four hundred dollars!

It was more money than John Cavendish could imagine. He didn't know what Luke had done to make so much money — and he suspected it probably hadn't been easy — but there it was, written down in blue ink. And actually it was more than that. It was four hundred and two dollars and seventy-three cents, because Luke had been carrying the two seventy-three in change in his pocket.

Wainlodes had said that Doc Starling would be able to provide him with the death certificate. He wasn't sure that that alone would be enough to persuade the bank to sign over the money. Maybe Luke's letters, and his original contracts of employment and dismissal from the Pinkertons — proving who he was — would do it. They could even wire Guggenheim if needs be. But all that was for later.

First of all he wanted to see where Luke had died.

★ ★ ★

He leaned on his cane and looked along the alleyway. It was no place to die. No place special, that was. A very narrow street with two-storey snow-bound buildings on either side. It was shrouded in shadows, and save for the thin band of sky — itself dark and ominous with heavy clouds — it felt closed in, like a prison yard. He and Luke had grown up in an area full of such alleyways. They had loved running through that maze, but had also talked about breaking free. Luke had done so, and had then been dragged back to such a place to die.

Had it been the wrong place at the wrong time? If Luke had been there a minute earlier would everything have been different? But wasn't that life? Had he been a step faster back in the cut then the metal pole would have missed him and he'd still be working for the Pinks.

He found a café halfway down the alleyway. He went in and drank coffee and ate bread and beans. He spoke to everyone he could, and asked about the killings. No one had seen anything. A few — including the girl doing the cooking in the café — had heard the shots and seen the aftermath, but there were no actual witnesses.

Later he limped back out and tried the other businesses, and one private home, along the alleyway.

Nothing.

Maybe there was nothing to be discovered. Maybe it truly had been the way people said. But the Pinkerton in him insisted that he dig deeper and question harder. Most of all, it just felt too random.

There was more snow falling. It gave Julesville a pretty veneer. Everything looked clean. Wheel-tracks and hoof-marks had been filled in. If you stood still and it was a moment when not too many people were moving it almost looked like a painting from one of the galleries back east.

He shivered and pulled his collar tighter. Breath frosted in clouds around his mouth. His knee ached. His hand was hurting where he gripped the cane-head. His left shoulder protested where he had compensated for the other pains in his body.

He wanted to rest, somewhere inside where it was warm, somewhere he didn't have to lower his head against the icy wind. But first he would go and find the doc, and then see what the bank had to say about Luke's fortune.

19

Caleb Stone couldn't speak. The echoes of the gunshot refused to die, bouncing back and forth off the kitchen walls and doing the same within his head. His heart, too, was hammering as loudly as those echoes.

I thought I was about to die.

Somehow he managed to stand, albeit on trembling knees. He looked down at Flynn. There was no doubt the man was dead. Blood pooled about his body, soaking into his clothes, running between the cracks of the boards on the floor. The coppery smell of all that blood hung in the air, along with cordite and gunpowder, the smoke from the stove and the cigarettes, the cooking.

Leaping Fox was looking at him, his gun lowered now. A string of smoke rose from the barrel.

Stone took a deep breath, held it, and exhaled slowly.

'He wanted me to kill you,' Leaping Fox said.

Stone looked at him. 'I thought you were going to.'

Leaping Fox smiled. 'We're on the same side. He told me that. He told you, too.'

'Yes.'

'Anyway, we want those guns. Whiskey?'

Stone was suddenly too hot. He shrugged the big coat off his shoulders and hung it on the back of a free chair. He sat down again.

'Thank you.'

Stone drank the whiskey that Leaping Fox offered him. He pulled out his makings and started to roll a cigarette. His fingers were trembling.

'He thought these guns would bring too much trouble. Bring inspectors or the army or . . . I don't know. He thought it would ruin the whiskey trade, and the rifle trade.'

Stone focused on his cigarette. He said nothing. He willed his fingers to be steady.

'He wasn't happy about you shooting Rudy. He said you were losing control.'

Stone looked up. He flicked a Lucifer into life and lit his cigarette.

'What are you going to do now?' Stone asked.

'Me?'

'Uh-huh.' Stone breathed deeply. The smoke felt good in his lungs. He could feel himself calming down. 'About him.' Stone nodded at Flynn's body.

'I'll hide him outside.'

'And if anyone comes?'

'No one comes here in winter, Caleb. Only you and the men delivering your whiskey and guns. I will live here. You can deliver me whiskey as normal. You bring the big guns, too, when they arrive. By the time anyone finds out Flynn is dead it will all be too late, anyway.'

★ ★ ★

Sam Loude's shack was on the south side of the railroad yard, where hundreds of similar cabins had sprung up as Julesville had expanded. These cheap shacks had been built in a random manner, and together they created a maze of muddy tracks and alleyways, with just a cross of two wider roads cutting the area into quarters. Arkansas Joe and African Joe lived in the north-east quarter, as did Cal, whereas Sam's cabin was in the south-west quadrant. All of them now had enough money to move into boarding houses on the other side of the tracks if they desired, but none of them did. It was easier to get lost down here, to not be noticed.

Sam sat close to the tiny stove in the corner. He cradled a bottle of label-less whiskey in his lap. An oil lamp hung from a hook in the middle of the ceiling. He had a table, a cot, this chair, and a cupboard. His gun was unbelted, but it was within grabbing distance on the table. Down in the Quarters it didn't pay to stray too far from your gun.

He lifted the whiskey to his lips, and drank.

Sam had once read a battle report from the 'War Between the States'. He couldn't remember which battle, which year, or even which side won that day. What he could remember was the description of the dead and the dying, of how great cannonballs had ripped through the ranks of men, chewing them up like they were nothing but jerky, tearing off arms, legs and heads. After the battle was over a fire had raged through the dry undergrowth and many of those who had lain there terribly injured, unable to move, had burned to death or suffocated.

But there'd been something else, too. There had been new guns: Gatling guns. At one point in the battle a line of soldiers had marched forwards — just like they'd done a dozen times before — muskets and rifles and carbines extended before them, slowly closing in on the enemy, when these new guns had opened up. One soldier who had miraculously survived said the sound was like a hundred angry rattlesnakes, but magnified a thousand times. A whirring, a clicking, and a moment later a hundred men screamed and fell. The entire line was devastated in under a minute. There'd been nothing like it before. It was unimaginable and it was terrible.

Sam just couldn't figure that it was right for a good American to sell something like that to the Indians.

Oh, he had no investment in the army, emotional or any other way. He had a brother who had been in the cavalry — maybe still was. But it wasn't that. He wasn't thinking about saving his brother's life. It was bigger than that. The Indians were on the run. Sure, they won a battle or a stand here and there, but another year or so and the might of America would destroy them. It was how it was meant to be, and it would make things better for everyone.

But you start giving them Gatling guns, you give them an edge, and who knows where it could lead. Cal had started off selling them whiskey — which turned out to be a good thing, the way they got drunk and became incapacitated — and then rifles, and now this. Where would it end?

No, it wasn't right. But what could one man do?

He thought on it a little longer, drank some more whiskey — and the answer, he decided, was dynamite.

And he knew exactly where he could get some.

20

When he returned to his room late on Thursday, there was an additional blanket on his bed. It was folded and it lay on top of the bed like a present. Initially he thought that Mrs Beaumont must have put it there because the weather was so cold. He assumed she had one for each room, and he smiled at her thoughtfulness. But when he unfolded it to spread it out over the existing blanket he realized it was new — it smelled fresh and clean, and it was soft as if it had never been close to water.

He slept well, but sometime in the early hours he found himself in the strange zone between sleep and wakefulness, able to think and control those thoughts, but also standing at a distance observing them, as if the thoughts didn't quite belong to him.

The bank had been happy to sign over the money. The death certificate, the Pinkerton contracts, and the first letter from his brother had proved to be enough evidence of who he was. Especially as it turned out that William Wainlodes had already been in to testify on his behalf. He'd needed a little for the funeral, so he'd taken ten dollars from the account. It was the first withdrawal since his brother had set up the account almost four weeks before.

So Luke had been living on something else, John Cavendish thought, with the palest of colours starting to show in the night sky between his not-quite-closed curtains through his not-quite-closed eyes.

Two dollars, seventy-three cents, his half-dreaming mind whispered.

Was that a coincidence, too? Had Luke just about burned through all the rest of his money and was down to his last couple of bucks when the random bullet had killed him?

Unlikely.

In his half-awake state he wondered on the new blanket and the look of guilt that morning in Mrs Beaumont's eyes, standing there looking pretty in her new dress.

Look at her husband's boots, a distant part of his mind said. *When you get up this morning, check out Mr Beaumont's footwear.*

★ ★ ★

William Wainlodes had arranged for Luke's coffin to be taken to the cemetery on a flatbed wagon pulled by a white horse.

'We're best to walk behind,' he said. 'If you're OK to do so.'

'I might have a stick but I can walk,' John Cavendish said.

So it was that at ten-fifteen on that Friday, with enough snow in the air that John Cavendish had to keep blinking, he and Wainlodes walked silently through the snow behind the wagon on the short journey to the cemetery.

People stopped and bowed their heads as the small procession passed. Most of the men removed their hats.

'Do they know who he was?' Cavendish asked. 'I mean, do they know whose funeral this is?'

'I don't think many knew him,' Wainlodes said quietly. 'It's only a small town, but we have our ways. It takes a while to fit in. But they know it's him. They know the sheriff's body went out on the train.'

As they passed the bank Cavendish saw a young woman on the far plank-walk stop, turn, and stare. Although the snow blurred his vision he saw she was very pretty. She bowed her head and crossed herself. He smiled thinly at her. They walked on, his cane pressing through the snow searching for solid ground with every step.

A minute later Cavendish realized the woman had joined them, and was walking along behind him.

★ ★ ★

The priest, Father Edwards, said a few words and led the three of them — and the wagon driver, who was standing to one side looking unsure whether he was part of the funeral or not — in prayers. Father Edwards committed Luke's soul to God and his body to the ground, whilst all the while Luke rested on the back of the flat wagon.

Afterwards, William Wainlodes, Father Edwards, the wagon driver and John Cavendish — with his stick laid temporarily on the floor — managed to slide Luke's coffin from the wagon and place it on to a shelf within the stone mausoleum. There was just one other coffin inside the stone shelter, on a low shelf to the right.

Cavendish thanked the priest, and he thanked Wainlodes, who both climbed on to the wagon's bench for the short ride back into town.

Cavendish turned to the girl. She was wearing a red scarf tied beneath her chin and a black coat. There were snowflakes on her long eyelashes.

'Ella?' he said.

She looked surprised, her dark eyes widening, becoming even bigger.

'How did you know?'

'I'm a detective,' he smiled.

'A detective.' She nodded as if a connection had been made.

'Well, I was. Until . . .' He held up his walking stick.

'You're John, aren't you?'

'It's my turn to be impressed.'

Behind them, Cavendish heard the wagon driver call a quiet gee-up. He looked over as the wagon starting rolling back towards town. Wainlodes glanced back at him, and

Cavendish raised a hand in acknowledgement.

'Luke told me about you. He was so proud of you.'

'Proud, huh?'

'Oh, yes. His brother the Pinkerton. He didn't say . . . Well, I don't think he knew . . .' She nodded at his stick.

'I was pretty lax in returning his letters. How did you know him?'

She brushed snowflakes from her eyes. A slight wind was making the snow float and meander in the air on the way to the ground, where it drifted against wooden crosses and the raised mounds of frozen earth in the graveyard. 'Listen,' Cavendish said, before she had chance to respond. 'It's cold. Can I buy you lunch? I mean, if you're not busy. Save us standing here freezing.'

She smiled, and he felt a shiver in his shoulders that was nothing to do with the temperature. Grace aside, there had been no smiles from pretty women in a long time. It was a pleasant feeling, and in that moment he realized how much he'd missed it.

'Yes,' she said. 'That would be nice.'

★ ★ ★

They sat at the window table in a small eating house called The Gold Rush. The room was warm and the windows were misty with condensation. Outside the snow was picking up again. John

Cavendish ordered English tea, with toast and butter. Ella said she'd have the same. She untied her scarf, and her red hair fell to her shoulders. She shook her head to help her hair settle.

On the way from the cemetery to the café she'd told John Cavendish that she'd met Luke right here in Julesville. 'On the street, actually,' she'd said. 'I was looking in the window of that shop down by where . . .' She'd paused and Cavendish realized she was referring to a shop just along from the alleyway where Luke had been killed. 'I know the one,' he'd said. She'd smiled, and continued, 'I was looking in the window at a pretty dress and I heard a voice say 'It would suit you, ma'am.' That was it. He was charming and very . . . boyish. He had a cheeky smile, really a grin, and he was full of life. We met a few times.'

Now, in the window seat of The Gold Rush, she asked John Cavendish what he'd done to his leg.

He told her the story of the strike-breaking job he'd been assigned to.

'I'm not proud,' he said. 'I should have told them no. I've never been . . . *against* the workers. It's just . . .'

She must have seen some anguish in his eyes because she reached out and placed a hand on his.

'It's what?' she said.

It was his turn to shake his head. Not to settle his hair, but to clear his mind.

'It's nothing. I've only just met you. I don't need to burden you with my dark side.'

'We've all got a dark side.'

He smiled and blinked. Whenever he ventured close to the memories of his father, and the sacrifices John senior had made so the family could eat, he found tears springing to his eyes. 'I can't imagine you have a dark side.'

'You'd be surprised.'

'Surprise me, then.'

The lady, Agnes, who ran The Gold Rush, brought over a tray of cups and plates, some knives, a jug of milk and a dish of butter. 'The rest is coming,' she said.

'Looks nice,' Ella said to Agnes. 'Thank you.'

When Agnes had gone, Cavendish smiled at Ella. 'What brings you here? I guess you're not married?'

'You wanted to know about my dark side?' She leaned forwards conspiratorially, and he saw her eyes were actually green, dark green speckled with brown. Her lips shone and her cheeks were smooth, although he saw one cheek was bruised. 'I've come to kill my husband,' she whispered.

She stared at him, still leaning forwards. He held her gaze. He was aware of Agnes coming back, this time with a teapot and two plates of toast.

'You are married, then,' he said, as Agnes put the food down on the table between them.

Ella leaned back. She smiled.

'Yes, I am. Hopefully not for long. It's not the response I was expecting.'

'What were you expecting?'

'I don't know. Do you believe me?'

'Tell me why. Tell me about it.'

'This is a little bit crazy. I see your brother in you — the same eyes, the same mouth. He was younger, wasn't he? And I'd say he was a little wilder — maybe more boyish, as if he'd never quite grown up. You're more serious. But because he and I walked out a few times, several times, I feel like I know you. I shouldn't have said what I did. Pretend I was joking.'

'But you weren't joking, were you?'

She placed a piece of toast on her plate, took a knife and started buttering the toast.

'Milk?' he asked.

'Yes.'

He poured for them both. The steam from the cups rose up between them.

'I've got a gun,' she said. 'Back at Angelina's — my landlady. I don't carry it much. But it's there. I told Luke, and I told Angelina. I told them how Reuben — my husband — left me holding a baby and lit out for the Black Hills with a girl by the name of Pearl. She was fourteen. Maybe fifteen. I don't know. Young enough that it wasn't her fault. Reuben was chasing gold, and he was selling Pearl a dream about a life that he had no right to sell her.'

He wanted to say that Pearl must have been very pretty indeed, but he sipped the scalding tea and said nothing.

'When he lit out with her I was mad as hell, and I was upset, and I was all those things you'd expect. I called him a bastard, although he wasn't there to hear it, and I tried to figure out what I'd done wrong or what I hadn't done right. But I came to realize that some men are just that way. They can't settle for what they have. They can't stick with their promises and their duties. There's always something better. I wouldn't be surprised if he hasn't left Pearl in some hovel somewhere on the trail, the same as he did for me, and lit out with another young pretty one. But the thing is . . .'

She paused, the buttered toast untouched. He saw her eyes were wet. Her hand was resting on the table where she'd put down the knife.

'My baby. *Our* baby. Reuben's and mine. It died. *She* died. I had no money and I did my best, but the poor little thing... Charlotte. She caught the flu and there was nothing I could do. We didn't have enough to eat. She wasn't strong enough to fight it. *That* tore my heart out. After Charlotte died I was different. I knew something had died within me. It was then that I knew Reuben would have to die, too.'

He reached out and placed his hand on hers.

'I'm sorry,' he said.

'Thank you. But it's not for you to be sorry.'

'Is he here? In Julesville?'

'Uh-huh. I looked all over. It wasn't easy and I've had some scary times. But this is where the trail led.'

'You're a detective, too.'

She smiled. She drank some tea and she bit into her toast delicately.

'I saw him a few days back, for the first time. Down in the railroad yard. He was driving a wagon, loading and carrying goods, by the looks of it. Didn't look like he found any gold.'

'Did you speak?'

'No. I kept my distance. I have to figure out what to do.'

She lifted her tea to her lips again. The steam, rising around her face, looked ghostlike.

'Angelina, my landlady... You know, she lost her baby, too. She gives me a free room and feeds me like I was her child. It's because we've both lost babies. Well, Angelina doesn't think I can do it. She says I'm too nice.'

'Maybe she's right.'

'She says that I'm no killer, and the way I acted back when... when your brother was killed, proves it. The way I tried to grab hold of the killer...'

'Wait a minute, you were there?'

'Yes.'

'You saw it? You saw my brother get shot?'

★ ★ ★

The quartermaster, Westlake, counted the money, nodded, and said, 'The guns will be on the noon train, Monday. They'll be in the last wagon before the caboose. You take them all off as usual, and then bring two — along with all the other stuff for the Fort to me. The other two . . .' He shook his head. 'I shouldn't be doing this.'

'Two hundred dollars,' Caleb Stone said. 'Right there in your hand. A year's pay, I'd wager. Plus all that you've made so far on the rifles. *That's* why you're doing it.'

'I'm done, though.'

'I know. I am, too. After this I'm gone.'

'You are?'

Stone watched Westlake tuck the sheaf of money inside his coat. His hands were shaking.

'I'm headed south,' he said. 'The sun must be shining somewhere. I'm going where it's warm and where no one knows me.'

Now Westlake's teeth were chattering.

'You scared?' Stone said. 'Or cold?'

They were, as usual, in the back of the relay station where the horses stood shivering even under blankets. They could hear the wind whistling over the stable roof, and somewhere a loose window shutter banged.

'Relieved,' Westlake said.

'That's all?'

'OK, I'm scared, too. And I'm not afraid to admit it. I should never have got into this. But it's done now. Most of all I don't like the fact that you know what I've done. You understand?'

Stone nodded. That was exactly how he felt. It was one thing stepping away from everything and heading south, but there would always be people who knew. People who had been involved. And it seemed that the number was always growing.

'You could shoot me,' he said, looking Westlake in the eye. Truth be told, he'd wondered if that's why Westlake had been shaking. Had the quartermaster been waiting for the money and then been going to draw a gun from beneath his coat?

'I guess I could. But we're partners, aren't we?'

Stone smiled. The man was naïve. But it was nice that someone in the deal actually felt that being a partner meant something.

Stone thought of Flynn's body, up at the other station, buried in the snow, where he and Leaping Fox had dragged it, a long smear of blood against the whiteness. A smear that was almost covered by the time he had left.

'Plus you said you'd got it all written down. Not that I believe you.'

'It's been good dealing with you,' Stone said.

'Really?'

'Really.'

The truth was, now that everything was lined up, Stone had actually considered killing Westlake. Maybe following him at a distance until they were somewhere deserted between the relay station and the fort, and doing it there. Burying the body in snow like they had Flynn, and not having to worry about what happened after the melt as he'd be long gone, just like Leaping Fox had said. The trouble was, he wasn't sure that Westlake didn't have to wire confirmation or something to the depot back east. Plus he needed Westlake to sign for receipt of goods when Reuben took the legitimate stuff down to the fort.

No, much as he hated loose ends, he had to let Westlake live.

The way he was feeling though, the way the hairs on his neck seemed to bristle with warning every day, he hated to leave people alive.

★ ★ ★

'Yes, I saw it all,' Ella said.

John Cavendish put down his cup. His hands were trembling.

'What happened? I've not been able to find anyone who was there.'

'It was coincidence. I wasn't there because of Luke. I was walking by the alleyway and I had no idea he was down there. I heard a gunshot and I looked to my left and I saw the sheriff fall. That's when I realized the man standing between the sheriff and the shooter was Luke. Luke was turning, he looked as surprised as anyone, and then the man shot him as well.'

A tear ran from her left eye. She wiped it away.

'I'm sorry,' she said.

'No, *I'm* sorry. Are you all right to talk about this?'

'Yes, of course. It was just . . . I liked your brother. He was fun.'

'Yes, he always was. You said earlier you tried to grab hold of the killer. Who was he? I mean . . . I know *who* he was. Wainlodes told me that it was someone named Rudy Oliver. A deserter. Wainlodes said the posse trailed him and shot him.'

'He was just a youngster as far as I could tell. He looked scared. I tried to grab him, but he kicked me. Here.' She touched her cheek.

'You said he shot the sheriff first.'

'Yes.'

'You saw the sheriff fall?'

'Yes.'

'And then, only after the sheriff had fallen, did he shoot Luke?'

'Yes.'

'Everyone has said it was a ricochet.'

'No. There were two shots.'

'The first one killed the sheriff, and the second one killed Luke.'

'Yes.'

'Then the intention wasn't to kill the sheriff,' Cavendish said. 'The intention was to kill Luke.'

21

On his way back to see William Wainlodes, John Cavendish couldn't get Ella Scarr out of his mind. It wasn't just Ella, it was what she'd said. And it wasn't just what she'd said about the killing, it was what she'd said about herself. It all spun around inside his head like a snow-storm buffeted by a whirlwind. The way she'd looked at him, with those green and brown eyes, that bruise on her cheek, the way she'd held his hand. His heart raced just thinking of her. It had been so long since he'd felt such an immediate attraction to a woman. Then there was her past — not just her past with Luke, which he still wasn't sure about, but the fact she was married and, supposedly, planning to kill her errant husband. Although, like Ella's landlady, Angelina, he couldn't imagine Ella as a killer.

And on top of all of this was the fact that Luke's killing had been deliberate.

Or so it seemed. If the killer — Rudy Oliver — had been targeting the sheriff, why would he have shot Luke? It couldn't have been because Luke had been a witness — or if it was, why hadn't he shot Ella, too? No, Luke had stumbled upon a scheme that he thought would make him easy money, he had sounded out the key players, and then he had been shot.

The starting point was Rudy Oliver.

'Who was the young lady?' William Wainlodes asked him. 'She was very pretty.'

They were back in Wainlodes's kitchen, with the stove warming the room, and this time drinking French brandy rather than coffee. Cavendish explained who Ella was, without going into details on much of what she'd shared with him. He thanked Wainlodes for organizing his brother's funeral. Then he asked: 'The other coffin up there, in the mausoleum. Who is it?'

Wainlodes pursed his lips.

'I've got nowhere else to put them this weather. That's Rudy Oliver. I'm sorry they have to be together.'

'I'm not superstitious or anything. So they brought Rudy to you.'

'Yes, they did.'

'Do you know anything about him? Did he have anything on him?'

Wainlodes sipped the French brandy.

'No and no. His pockets were empty. The posse brought him in and dumped him with the sheriff — well, Jack Byron. He's the deputy. Acting sheriff now, I guess. Jack came and got me. But anything the kid had on him, his gun, money . . . I don't know. Jack will have it.'

'You didn't know him?'

'No. Why the interest in Rudy all of a sudden, John?'

'I think my brother was the target, not the sheriff.'

★ ★ ★

Jack Byron was tall and lean. His brown hair was barbered short and he was clean shaven. There was a scar on one cheek, and his blue eyes were bright and more than happy to hold John Cavendish's gaze. Byron was wearing blue jeans and brown boots — without spurs — and even inside his office he had on an outdoor coat. He had a gun on his hip, and Cavendish made a mental note that maybe it was time he started belting on his gun again.

'You're Luke Cavendish's brother, huh?' Byron said, after John Cavendish had introduced himself. 'And Luke was the fellow got caught in the crossfire, Monday?'

'There wasn't any crossfire,' Cavendish said. 'There were two shots. Rudy Oliver shot the sheriff, and then he shot my brother.'

'Well, if that's what you say. Thing is, Rudy's dead, so you can rest easy. Caleb Stone tracked him up to an old hunter's lodge. Rudy — you'd have thought a soldier would know better — left tracks in the snow that a dead dog could follow.'

'I know he's dead. May I sit down? This leg... It feels like I've been walking all day, and in this weather it kills me.'

'Sure. Take a seat. What happened to your leg?'

'A little trouble with an iron bar.'

Jack Byron winced. He sat down behind his desk and pulled open the bottom drawer. 'You want a drink?'

'No, I'm OK, thank you.'

'Mind if I do?'

'Carry on.' Cavendish pulled out a chair and sat down opposite Byron.

'So, what can I do for you?' Byron asked, pouring an amber drink from an unlabelled bottle.

'I've got a witness...'

'Wait a minute. You've got a *witness*? Who did you say you were? You a prosecutor or something?'

'No. I'm a brother, that's all. Sorry. Before this,' Cavendish tapped his knee. 'Before I was hurt I was a Pinkerton.'

'A Pink, huh?'

'And the training kicks in. Like any brother, I want to know who killed Luke, and why.'

'I can tell you why. Rudy heard that Clyde — that's Clyde Johnson, the sheriff that Rudy shot — had figured where Rudy was living and was about to turn him into the army. You know he was a deserter?'

'Yes.'

'Well, Rudy heard this and came up here and shot Clyde. Seems like your brother Luke got caught in the exchange, whether it was a one-shot ricochet, two shots, or a cross-fire.'

'And where was Rudy living?'

'Far as I can tell he moved around. Back in the summer and autumn I figured he must have been up in the woods — maybe in that shack where Caleb shot him. In the winter I'd guess he pulled his scarf up and his hat down and maybe lived with friends down in the Quarters.'

'Clyde never said?'

'I'm not sure Clyde knew. I think Rudy got it into his head that he did. But that don't mean anything. Fellow deserts from the army and then sticks around ten miles from where he was based doesn't say much for his thinking.

Like I just said, at a guess I'd say he was probably living in that mess of shacks the other side of the railroad yard. The Quarters. It's an easy place to get lost.'

'Did you know him? I mean, did you see him around town? Know who his friends were?'

Byron leaned back in his chair, resting his drink — whiskey or brandy or whatever it was — on his chest. 'You sure ask a lot of questions.'

'Sorry, as I said, it's what I was trained for.'

'Hmmm.'

Cavendish held the man's gaze.

Byron said, 'No. After they brought the body in I sort of recognized him. I guess I'd seen him around. But I don't recall who he rode with, if anyone.'

'What happened to his things?'

'His horse is down the livery racking up bills that we'll have to sell the horse to pay. His saddle and bags are down there, too. There wasn't much in them. I have his gun. It's army property and I guess they'll want it back some day.'

'Nothing else?'

Byron leaned forwards.

'Listen, I'm a patient man, Mr Cavendish. I'm not sure what you're after. This killing was what it was — Rudy wanted to kill Clyde, and your brother was in the wrong place at the wrong time. Sure, you 'have a witness'. It doesn't mean anything. You say Rudy fired two shots? Maybe he panicked. Or maybe the army trains them to fire twice to make sure — I don't know. I appreciate your position, but I think we're done here.'

★ ★ ★

By late afternoon, John Cavendish was aching too much to walk down to the railroad yard and the Quarters beyond. His left knee, thigh, wrist and shoulder had all been complaining for hours, and now his ankles had joined in, too. The snow had relented, although the day was already darkening and it was hard to tell if the sky was heavy with snow or if it was simply dusk moving in. With the darkness came a drop in temperature and he had started shuddering with cold.

Wearily, he stamped the snow from his boots outside the Beaumonts' boarding house and went inside. The house was warm and the smell of cooking came from the kitchen. Cavendish made to head straight upstairs, but Mrs Beaumont opened the kitchen door.

'Mr Cavendish,' she said. 'You must be frozen. Would you like some stew? It's hot.'

She was wearing the new dress he'd first seen her in the previous day. Next to her stood Brian Beaumont. He was a short man with dark black hair and a nervous expression. His cheek fluttered as if something was alive just beneath the skin. His black trousers looked new. His shoes were definitely so, and John Cavendish recalled the thought that had crossed his mind in the hinterland between sleep and wakefulness that morning.

'The stew smells lovely and, yes, I'm frozen,' he said.

'Sit down . . . sit next to the stove and I'll pour you a dish.'

Cavendish didn't move.

'Sit down,' Mr Beaumont said. 'I've had some myself and it's terrific.'

'Nice shoes,' Cavendish said.

The tic in Beaumont's cheek danced.

'Thank you for the blanket, too. It felt brand new.'

Mrs Beaumont glanced briefly at her husband. 'It was,' she said.

'I went through my brother's things,' he said. 'The stuff you packed up and gave to William Wainlodes.' He looked at Brian Beaumont.

'Yes,' Beaumont said. It was neither question nor answer.

'There was no money,' Cavendish said. 'I mean, I'm sure you saw that he had a deposit book newly drawn on the bank right here in town.'

Beaumont nodded. His face reddened a little.

'But he hadn't touched any of that

money,' Cavendish said. 'I couldn't help but wonder what he was living on? He had two dollars seventy-three cents in his pocket. It's not a lot, is it?'

Mrs Beaumont gripped her dress at the throat. 'What are you suggesting?'

'There's a fellow runs a shop in town — a Rye Brewer. In the window of his shop he had a dress just like the one you're wearing now. Different colour — you may have seen it? Blue and cream. Yours is new, isn't it?'

'Yes.'

'He had a selection of shoes, too. I asked Mr Brewer if you were good customers of his. You know, did you buy much? He said . . .'

'Look,' Mr Beaumont said. 'There was some money. Not a lot. Not compared to what he'd put in the bank. But a lot compared to what we've got. I didn't know you were coming. I didn't know *anyone* was coming. I figured . . .'

'You stole the money.'

'I figured the bank would get to keep all that money he deposited, and probably someone else, I don't know, maybe Wainlodes...'

'William Wainlodes is an honest man.'

'Well someone would have had it! Wainlodes would have given it to Jack Byron. He's the deputy...'

'I know who he is. I've been to see him.'

'You've been to see him?' There was fear on Brian Beaumont's face. His wife's knuckles were white where she gripped the collar of her dress.

'Not about you.'

'Look...someone would've had it. We just felt...'

'You stole my brother's money.'

'I'm sorry. I can pay you back what we've got...'

'Keep it,' Cavendish said. 'Keep your stew, too. I'll take my stuff and I'll be gone within fifteen minutes. I can't stay here a moment longer.'

Cavendish turned. At the kitchen door he stopped and looked back at the two of them.

'You know, maybe I should go back

and see Byron again? He and I were wondering on motive — maybe you arranged for Luke to be killed just to get that money?' Cavendish knew it wasn't true. They didn't have it in them for such a plot, and whatever money they would've gained would've been scarcely worth the risk.

'No,' Mr Beaumont said, shaking his head. 'I swear. No.'

'You're lucky,' Cavendish said. 'I know people who would shoot you for what you've done.'

★ ★ ★

The Black Hills gold rush had been raging since Custer — God rest his good American soul — and his troops had found the first gold four years back. Many followed in Custer's footsteps, and for a couple of years the lucky ones found gold in the creeks and streams just by lifting and sieving shovel-loads of earth. But then the clever ones realized that all this loose gold must be getting washed down from somewhere, and if they could find that somewhere, why, then they'd be rich.

And that was exactly what happened. A group of fellows led by Fred and Moses Manuel found the source and set up a mine, and sure enough, when they sold the mine on to some folks from back east a year or so later, they became rich beyond all imaginings. The thing was, an awful lot of other folks were looking for something similar, and Rye Brewer got ahead of the game and figured he'd make just as much money from selling these prospectors tools and provisions, as they were liable to make from the gold. Truth was, Rye Brewer probably made more.

One of the things Rye Brewer offered to sell these prospective miners was dynamite.

Sam Loude didn't know where Rye had sourced the dynamite — maybe he did what Cal was doing with guns, or maybe he just placed an order, the way he did with shoes or soap or horse feed.

However he did it, Sam knew that Rye had some dynamite.

It was time to buy a few sticks off him.

★ ★ ★

Caleb Stone walked through the slush and mud in the dark alleyways of the Quarters, both shivering and sweating beneath his trapper's fur coat. It felt as if the place was closing in on him. Everyone he saw seemed to have malevolence and mischief in their eyes. He nodded at some and grunted greetings at others, but couldn't shake the feeling that there was knowledge behind all those eyes. Knowledge about him. Maybe the thing to do was just to walk away. Do it now. Go back to the shack and pick up what few possessions he had, then head back across the rails to the livery, saddle up, settle up, and just go.

But there were one thousand reasons not to.

The train was due in Monday. Three days. He could be gone by Monday night or Tuesday morning. He just had to keep his wits about him for a few more days. His wits and his nerves. He'd been feeling it since before that incident up at the agent's office. But knowing that Flynn had intended shooting him there and then made a man feel vulnerable. When your friends started turning on you, where do you turn to?

The answer was, he decided, yourself.

Someone was walking towards him down the snow-lined alley. Beyond them he could see the railroad yard, a locomotive steaming, the silhouettes of buildings against the grey sky that looked lighter than normal even though it was full of snow clouds, smoke rising from chimneys, and a fire burning down by the side of the tracks. He eased open his coat and rested his hand on his gun.

Trust no one. That was how it was going to be for the next few days.

'Caleb,' the approaching man said, as he drew level. 'Cold one, ain't it?' Then the man was gone and Stone breathed out a cloud of air.

He could see The Engineer over on the other side of the yard. A couple of whiskies there, brief the two Joes and Sam, and that would do it. He'd head home and try and get to sleep whilst imagining what one could do with the best part of a thousand dollars way down in Mexico.

★ ★ ★

They sat at the Engineer's one table, close to the stove, the lamp surrounded by a bottle and four glasses of whiskey. The bar was two deep with yard-hands and engineers, men from the Quarters, and a few from the good side of the tracks who preferred the night-time anonymity of the Engineer. In the warmer seasons there was sometimes a girl or two, usually hanging around outside. But in winter the pleasures of the flesh were the last thing on the drinkers' minds. Staying warm was all that mattered. George poured drinks and handed out bottles, all the time registering and remembering who was having what, who paid, who owed, and who to refuse.

'You boys OK?' Caleb Stone said.

'Why wouldn't we be?' Sam Loude said. He stared across the table at Cal, conscious of African Joe and Arkansas Joe being right there, and of what he'd said to them when drunk earlier that week.

'Just asking. You know, after what happened to Rudy and all.'

'Did he have to die?' Arkansas Joe said, an unlit cigarette wedged in the gap between his teeth.

Stone nodded. 'Yes, he did.'

'He drew on you,' African Joe said. Sam had been about to say the same thing, but after the drunk session earlier in the week he was trying to keep his thoughts to himself. He'd already revealed too much to the Joes. He hoped they'd put it down to the whiskey.

'Uh-huh. I don't know why. I told him not to, too.'

'Maybe he could see the future,' Sam said.

'How's that?' Stone said. He stared at Sam, and Sam wondered if either of the Joes had said anything to him.

'He'd killed two men. You and the posse had him cornered. What was going to happen? He wasn't going to walk away, was he?'

'I'd have figured something out. That's why I led the posse. Anyone else was likely to have hung him there and then.'

Both Joes were looking at him as if to say: *See, Cal had thought it through.*

'Maybe he'd seen men hanged in the army,' Sam said. 'Or maybe he remembered that story you told us, about good hanging and bad hanging.'

'It wasn't Cal's fault,' Arkansas Joe said, his eyes as hard and as dark as coal. 'Rudy should have trusted him.'

'Not saying it was. Just trying to figure out why he might have pulled on Cal.' Sam took a long drink of whiskey. He put the glass down, lifted the bottle, and topped up his drink. He stared back at Arkansas Joe.

'Fact is,' Stone said. 'He's dead. We're

not. And we've got the big one coming in next week.'

'Is it all sorted, boss?' African Joe said.

'Uh-huh. Monday at noon. The guns will be in the last wagon before the caboose.'

Sam could feel Arkansas Joe's stare still boring into him.

'I'll be there, boss,' Sam said, and took another drink of whiskey.

22

John Cavendish left The Horizon Hotel after breakfast and stepped out into a clear day, no snow in the air, no clouds in the sky. He turned towards the station, retracing his steps of several days before. The world had changed so much in those few days. His brother was dead — and buried. The killing had been, at least as far as Cavendish could tell, intentional rather than random. The murderer was dead, too, but the question of *why* weighed on Cavendish's mind. Then a seemingly good couple had proved to be thieves, taking the pennies from a dead man's eyes, as it were. And he'd met a woman who caused his heart to race and somehow make all this darkness bearable.

So much change, and yet everything was the same: the snowdrifts against the buildings, the wet and muddy road, the smoke rising from every chimney. In the distance, yardmen dressed in heavy winter clothes rushed about moving crates and boxes and sacks.

He walked to the yard now, leaning lightly on his stick. First thing in the morning his leg felt reasonably strong, but as the day progressed he knew he'd be putting more and more weight on the cane and up through his arm.

The plan was to wander down to the area known as the Quarters, the place where Rudy Oliver was likely to have lived. Maybe someone down there would know Rudy, would be able to shed light on why he might have shot Luke. Maybe there would be a lead into Rudy's world and Rudy's friends.

But Cavendish had another plan, too. He had Luke's photograph in his pocket. Sure, it was a younger Luke, but he was recognizable. Cavendish figured there'd be no harm in showing the photograph to whoever was down here. It might be another way into whatever trouble Luke had stumbled.

There was one other change, too, and

it made the first few minutes of his walk awkward as it took a little getting used to. He'd strapped on his Colt 45 again, for the first time since that night up in the Seventh Street cut.

★ ★ ★

The man, whose name was Ray, said, 'Yeah, I saw him a few times. Spoke to him once. Who is he?'

Ray was the third fellow to whom Cavendish had shown the photo as he had wandered from the station building, across the railroad yard, edging towards the Quarters.

'He's my brother. You spoke to him, you say?'

'Uh-huh. A few weeks ago he came down here looking for work. Well, I say looking for work, I don't think he had much interest in doing this.' As he spoke, Ray lifted a bag of something from a flat-bed wagon and put it on the ground by his feet. 'I don't think he was interested in hard work, if you know what I mean?

No offence.'

'What was he looking for?'

'My guess is that he'd heard there was a few . . . what shall we say . . . *deals* to be had. There always is around yards like this. I think he was looking for a way in.'

'Did you give him any?'

'No. I keep out of it. I do the regular stuff, and that's all.'

'And you saw him again?'

'Uh-huh. Just a few days ago he was back down here. I wondered if I'd read him wrong and he really was looking for work. I mean, he didn't look like he needed work, but you never know. I see the resemblance now, with you.

They're good, aren't they? These photographs.'

'And what was he doing just a few days ago?'

'Dunno. We didn't speak. He went straight into the Engineer.' Ray nodded towards the dark shack over at the far end of the yard. 'Guess he knew who he was looking for.'

'Do you know who that might have

been?'

'Like I said, I keep out of it. But go and ask George — you can't miss him, he's only got one eye. But he sees everything.'

★ ★ ★

One-Eyed George said, 'Nope, never seen that fellow in my life.' John Cavendish said, 'Maybe someone else runs the counter sometimes?' George said, 'You're new here, huh?'

'Yes.'

'Well, this is my bar. If it's open, then I'm running it.' 'And he's never been here?'

'You doubting my word now?'

'Just making sure we're understanding each other.'

'Who is the fellow, anyway?'

'My brother.'

'Brother, huh? And you've lost him?'

'He was shot dead up in town last Monday.'

'Ah, that fellow. I never saw him. But I heard about it.'

'Maybe you know the man that did it? A Rudy Oliver. The posse shot him dead.'

'No, I don't know Rudy. I mean, I heard about it and I heard about him. But I don't know him. I mean, I *didn't* know him.'

'He lived in the Quarters, so they tell me.'

'Who tells you?'

'Jack Byron.'

'You been talking to Jack, huh? You're asking a lot of people a lot of questions.'

'Someone shot my brother.'

'I heard that Rudy shot the sheriff and it was a ricochet killed your brother.'

'Then you heard wrong.'

'I did, huh?'

'Uh-huh.'

'You want a piece of advice, whatever you said your name was?'

'John Cavendish.'

'You want a piece of advice, John Cavendish?'

'I've a feeling I'm getting one whether I want it or not.'

'Maybe you shouldn't be asking so many questions. Maybe you should just leave things be.'

'Do you know something?'

'No. Leastways, not about what you're asking. But I know you're liable to rile up a few people going about things the way you are.'

'What people?'

'You don't let up, do you?'

'No.'

'I'm done answering your questions. You want a drink then that's fine, otherwise it's time to leave my bar.'

'In that case I'll have a drink.'

'I was afraid you'd say that. It's whiskey or whiskey.'

'I'll have whiskey.'

John Cavendish watched One-Eyed George lift an unlabelled bottle from below the counter and fill a shot glass.

'Don't worry about the finger marks on the glass,' George said. 'They're on the outside. It's on the house. Drink that and go. That's another piece of advice.'

★ ★ ★

George had been lying. John Cavendish knew that. There'd been a flicker of recognition in his eye when he had seen the photo — and anyway, Cavendish knew that Luke had been in The Engineer at least once. So George was hiding something, or covering for someone. He'd known Rudy, too. And he'd known exactly who would be upset at him asking questions about Luke's killing.

Which was interesting, because it meant there were people still alive who had an interest in the murder.

It meant that someone other than Rudy had been involved.

23

It had only happened twice. Well, twice here in Nebraska territory. The first time had been in the low hills a few miles north of Flynn's place — or should that be Leaping Fox's place now? Caleb Stone hadn't known the fellow was a Yankee until he'd stopped by the fire where Cal was brewing some coffee and roasting a rabbit. Cal was out there because he needed to be on his own. It happened once in a while. A tension would build inside his head. He got to thinking about his ma and pa, about their farm, about how the Yankees burned it down in the war and forced his folks to move, and how in the end that killed them. Cal's thinking would get so he started to hate everyone a little, and he knew he wasn't nice to be around. So he took himself off into the wilderness, and he rode around and tried to rein in his thoughts.

The Yankee hadn't stopped talking.

He'd ridden up and dismounted and pretty much invited himself into Cal's camp, and he just talked and talked and talked. It got so Cal's head was going to explode. So he just said to the fellow at one point, 'You're a Yankee, huh?' The man had flashed him a wide grin and had said, 'Sure, I am. Proud to hell of it, too.' And Caleb Stone had shot him, just like that.

The second one, they'd been drinking in Flynn's kitchen, way back when even the rifles were still just a vague idea in Cal's mind, and that fellow, *that* Yankee, had turned up and had started talking, too. What was it with these Yankees, they liked to talk so much? This one wanted some food. Not to eat there and then, but to take with him. He said how he'd seen the stables out the back were being used as some kind of store, that there was enough produce — that's what he'd said, *produce* — that they wouldn't miss just a little. Hell, you could feed a town with what you've got there, he'd said.

It's for the Indians, Flynn had

explained. The Indians, the man had said, a note of disparagement in his voice. They won't mind. Hell, they won't have to mind. But Flynn had refused, and the man had got angry, and when he left they had watched him through the window, and sure enough he'd snagged a couple of bags of something from the store and had brazenly thrown them over the back of his horse.

'I hate Yankees,' Cal had said, and had saddled up his own horse. He'd killed the man about two miles from the station and brought back the bags of *produce*.

He could feel the tension rising in his head again. It started in his shoulders and it was like a warmth that became a stiffness. It was a pressure that worked its way up into the back of his head and then started pressing outwards like a headache that didn't hurt, but that just made the inside of his head feel like it wasn't big enough, like there wasn't room up there any longer to think things through properly. At the same time his stomach would start to ache, start to growl.

It was happening now. He was feeling a little nauseous. The muscles in his arms and legs felt weak and inconsequential. Everything simply felt wrong.

He knew it was because of Monday. The train. The last deal. The big guns.

He knew it was because too many people knew about him. Or at least that's how it seemed.

Maybe if it had been spring or summer or autumn, any damn time but winter, he could have ridden up on the ridge, found and befriended, temporarily, a Yankee. But the snow had just about put paid to that. Oh, he could get up there all right. But what was the chances of anyone else being stupid enough to be out riding?

No, he'd just have to sit this one out like a storm. Go down to the yard, give Reuben the heads-up about Monday, and then hit The Engineer to see George and drink some of the whiskey that he himself had shipped in. Stick around his own kind for a day or two.

Let the pressure ease.

★ ★ ★

Sam Loude said to Rye Brewer, 'Can you keep a secret?'

Rye Brewer smiled. 'That depends, son.'

'On what?'

'On what the secret is.'

'I want to buy something off you, but I don't want you telling no one.'

'I see.'

'Is that OK?'

Rye Brewer pursed his lips. He was a thickset man, wide across the shoulders and chest, with strong legs and arms. He wore a blue pin-striped vest over a light blue shirt; his sleeves were rolled up despite the cold that swept into his store every time someone opened the door. He'd been running the shop for several years now, had seen the good times keep getting better, but he'd also had to be tough on many occasions. It wasn't any place for a man who wasn't prepared to stand up to others when the occasion demanded.

'Well, son, I can't think of anything I've got in my store that would be of much interest when it comes to knowing what other folks are buying, and yet only yesterday I had a fellow in here asking about other people's buying habits. But that aside, you buy what you want and my lips are sealed. What is it you want?'

Sam looked around. The shop was empty. He said, 'Dynamite. Dynamite and fuses.'

'Dynamite! Well hell, I never saw that coming! What on earth makes you think I've got dynamite for sale?'

'*You* did,' Sam said. 'We were talking one night in the Nugget. You said as how you'd bought a crate way back for the miners, but struggled to get rid of it.'

'I did?'

'Uh-huh.'

'That was a long time ago.'

'You've still got it, though?'

'And why does this have to be a secret? You planning on blowing up the bank?'

Sam smiled. 'No.'

'What then?'

'I can't say.'

'You want me to sell you dynamite, you won't tell me for what, but it's got to be a secret?'

'What if I say I'm going to start a mine?'

'Round here? I'd say you were lying. You head on up to the Black Hills, then maybe. But you're not, are you?'

Sam sighed. 'Look, I can't say. All I will say . . . there's some bad stuff happening. I mean, real bad, but the dynamite can stop it. And there's something else: no one will get hurt. I promise you that, Rye. Without the dynamite then an awful lot of people are going to get hurt. I mean, die. With the dynamite, I can stop it all. I can stop it all, and no one will be hurt.'

'Well, you can be pretty convincing, son. I'll give you that.'

'You a patriot?'

'I'd say so.'

'Well I am, too. And that's part of it. So you still have some?'

'Oh yes,' Rye said. 'I still have some. But there's a little problem.'

* * *

Ella Scarr stood on the plank-walk and looked across at the Beaumont Boarding House. Yesterday John Cavendish had mentioned in passing that it was where he was staying. She wondered about going over there, knocking on the door and seeing if he was about. It was unlikely, she knew. He'd told her he wanted to keep investigating why someone had shot Luke. Questions and footwork, he'd said. Or had it been the other way round? She couldn't remember. But she did recall how she'd enjoyed his company. That was another reason not to go over. She remained resolute about what she was here to do — and right now she was on her way down to the railroad yard, that small gun in her pocket — and yet somehow the idea, and that resolution, felt like it was slipping away from her a little. Meeting John had somehow had an effect on her that was to do with living, not dying.

So today she had decided to go down

to the railroad yard again where she had seen Reuben. Only this time, if he was there, she wouldn't keep her distance.

This time she would do what she had come to do, before it slipped too far away from her.

She owed Charlotte that much.

★ ★ ★

The dynamite was frozen, Rye said. And it wouldn't work when it was frozen. That was the first problem. It was frozen, and it was in a crate full of sand and hay, and the crate was a couple of miles out of town. This weather was the second problem.

'Why didn't you just blow it all up?' Sam asked. 'I mean, I'm glad you didn't, but why didn't you?'

'That was actually my intent. The day I hid it I took some blasting caps and some fuses but I forgot the matches. Always intended going back. But you know what it's like, one thing, then another.'

'So it's frozen and it's a couple of miles

away. How much to buy, say, six sticks?'

Brewer said, 'You know anything about dynamite, son? Because let me tell you, you're probably going to kill yourself. The reasons I stopped bringing it in wasn't because people didn't want it, but because it was just too damn dangerous.'

'How so?'

'See, it leaks when you leave it a while. And the stuff it leaks, well, you only have to look at it and it blows up. And that sets off the dynamite and then . . . Then you're dead.'

'I didn't think it worked when it was frozen?'

'No, the dynamite doesn't. But the stuff it leaks — nitroglycerine. That'll still blow up in your face.'

'I'm guessing that never happened to you?' Sam smiled. 'On account of you're still alive.' Rye Brewer always was one for a tall tale and a little melodrama. The man was knowledgeable for sure, but most of what he said was to enable him to add a few cents or a dollar to whatever item he was trying to sell. Always looking for easy money, Rye.

Rye Brewer smiled. 'It's what I was told, and I was always very careful. You know, maybe I should just say 'no'.

Maybe I should just price it high enough that you're not interested.'

'OK, so it's frozen and it's probably leaked. If I take the sticks out of the crate . . .'

'*Carefully* . . .'

'If I *carefully* take the sticks out of the crate, then I'll be all right?'

'They also say you shouldn't let the dynamite freeze.'

'I thought you said it was already frozen?'

'Exactly. Where it is, this weather it'll be frozen.'

'And you said it wouldn't work when frozen?'

'Uh-huh.'

Sam looked over at the window. Beyond a pretty dress and a nice rifle displayed in the window, he could see snow on the buildings opposite. The air, even inside Rye's shop, was the temperature of ice.

'See, when it's frozen you then have to thaw it to make it work,' Rye Brewer said.

'Right.'

'And then it's dangerous.'

'Isn't that exactly the point?' Sam was getting a bit frustrated. All he wanted to do was buy some dynamite. He had suspected Rye would lead him on a dance, but this was ridiculous.

'What I mean . . . what they say is, that once it's been frozen and thawed, then you have to be more careful than if it was never frozen in the first place.'

'Seems to me that it's a wonder all the miners in Dakota don't blow themselves up every winter.'

'Some of 'em do. And it won't be easy to thaw, this weather,' Brewer said. 'I don't recommend putting it too close to a fire. Maybe if your room is warm you just leave it there for a day.'

'I can do that.'

'But you need to be careful.'

'You keep saying.'

'Ten dollars,' Rye said. 'For whatever you find up there. You can take it all. I'll throw in a box of blasting caps and some slow-burning fuses, too. Five minutes, each.' Brewer nodded to himself as if remembering a long-gone decision. 'I had no idea what the miners would want. So that's what I ordered.'

'And where is 'there'?'

'Ten dollars.'

Sam pulled out a roll of bank notes and peeled several off the top.

'Much obliged. One moment.'

Brewer walked over to his cash box, which was bolted to his counter. He took a key from a pocket, unlocked the box, put the money in, and relocked the box. Then he walked further along the counter, reached down and picked up something. He came back along the counter.

'Where you're going, you'll need this. You bring it back, though.'

Brewer placed a long-handled shovel on the counter between them.

'Where is it?' Sam asked.

Rye Brewer said, 'The crate is at the back of the old store shed out at Vista Quarry.'

'Vista,' Sam said. 'That's not so far.'

There wasn't actually a quarry at Vista Quarry. A few folks, back when Julesville had been young, had figured that to save bringing in building materials from all over maybe they could source some closer to home. They'd tried quarrying in several places looking for good stone, but hadn't found any. Vista had been the one place that had been worked the longest and there were still a few old buildings there, some holes in the ground, and pretty much nothing else.

'I figured I needed a place where no one was ever likely to go,' Rye Brewer said. 'But if they did, they might at least expect to find some explosives there. The box is clearly labelled. Just remember what I told you.'

'Which bit?' Sam said.

'All of it.'

★ ★ ★

Ella watched Reuben heaving sacks from a flatbed cart on to a low platform that ran alongside one of the sidings in the middle of the yard. Two horses, one a grey and one jet black, were tethered to the cart, and their breath created great clouds in the cool afternoon air. A line of boxcars was on the far side of the platform. A couple of the boxcars just down from where Reuben was working had their doors open, and from where Ella stood she could see clear through one of them. She wondered why the doors on the non-platform side of the wagon were open. Maybe to let air in, she thought? Maybe to help dry out a damp wagon? The line of boxcars had no locomotive attached, but on another siding there was an engine being fired up, steam coming from down by the wheels, smoke from the funnel. There were men working on the locomotive, and a few more, like Reuben, unloading other carts. Over on the passenger platform a few people milled about.

Ella was wearing a dark scarf, and she pulled her collar up. Keeping her head bowed, she crossed a couple of tracks, at one point stepping into deep snow that came up over the ankles of her boots, and worked her way to the other side of a line of boxcars that were parked on rusting rails and looked like they hadn't moved in years. These old and damaged wagons gave her cover as she circled round to the far side of the train that Reuben was loading.

Her hand rested on the gun in her pocket. It was a small, five-shot pocket gun, which ironically Reuben had bought her. A Bulldog, he'd told her. Something she could, and should, carry in her bag.

She edged along the far side of Reuben's train. The palm of her hand was damp against the pistol grip. That morning Angelina had asked her where she was going, and when Ella had said she might try and find Reuben again, Angelina had smiled and suggested to her that they wander along Main Street, maybe see what Rye Brewer had new in store? Have lunch somewhere. That perhaps it was time to give up the fantasy about shooting Reuben. Gina said, hadn't she seen a man shot less than a week ago, and surely now that she knew what it was like, what it was really like . . . ?

Ella tried to keep her ragged breathing quiet as she edged along the far side of the wagons, getting closer and closer to the man who had killed their daughter. She tried to focus on the feelings and determination that had driven her for so long. She twisted her hand inside her pocket, trying to wipe the sweat away so that when the time came the gun wouldn't slip from her fingers.

★ ★ ★

Caleb Stone entered the yard by The Engineer, alongside George's railroad wagon home where the dog was barking and the cooking smelled good, and it was as if fate was on his side, because there, not forty yards from the door of the bar, was Reuben loading some freight on to a train.

Stone walked over to him.

'Reuben.'

'Caleb.'

'How's things?'

'Cold, tired and hungry. You?'

'About the same.'

'I've got the details about the next job,' Cal said.

'I'm listening.'

★ ★ ★

She was close enough that she imagined she could smell him. Smell that hot, musky scent that he'd always carried after a day's work. The smell of a working man, he'd told her one day, smiling, when she'd held him tight and kissed him and told him that she liked the way he smelled. But it was just imagination. She could see him through the open boxcar door, across the empty wooden boards of the boxcar floor where there was still some hay spread out as if it had been animals in there earlier, and through the open door on the other side. There he was, his back to her, as he moved those sacks from his wagon to the platform, his shoulders heaving with the effort, but making it look easy. But there was no smell other than that of coal smoke and her own fear.

She stopped by the edge of the open boxcar door and wiped her hand on the inside of her pocket. She slipped her fingers around the Bulldog.

She could hear him now, talking to someone who was just out of sight, and although it would have been easy — well, not easy, it would have been the hardest thing in the world — she could have pulled out that gun and lined it up on him, and squeezed the trigger. But no, she knew she had to see him, look him in the eye, and tell him why she was killing him. She needed to be closer, too. She had only ever fired the gun a half-dozen times, and to this day she had no idea where any of those bullets had gone.

So she pressed herself up against the

boxcar, and waited for Reuben and the other man to finish their conversation.

Then she would walk between the boxcars.

Then she would do it.

★ ★ ★

'Monday, at noon,' Caleb Stone said. 'You OK with that?'

'Sure,' Reuben said. 'I assume you'll be providing the drivers on account of it's one of *those* shipments?'

'Uh-huh. Sam and African Joe and you will take the stuff to the fort, me and Arkansas will take the rest up to the station.'

'Up to Flynn?'

'Ummm . . . Yes, up to Flynn.'

'Is it much stuff?'

'Not our bit of it. We'll be focusing on the last wagon.'

'Monday at noon,' Reuben said. 'I'll be here.'

★ ★ ★

She couldn't do it. She watched a big bearded man in a thick coat, which looked like it should have been on a mountain trapper, walk into sight, then turn and hold a hand up in acknowledgement to Reuben, and then walk out of sight. Reuben turned back to unloading the last of the sacks from his wagon.

She couldn't do it.

Her legs felt weak and her hand was wet again. Her throat was dry, and she pictured Luke Cavendish lying there in that alleyway, all that blood, that look of surprise in his unseeing eyes. She thought of his brother, battling with his stick, determined to find out who had killed Luke. Then she thought of Angelina and her unwavering belief that this was all a fantasy of Ella's, a fantasy that would play out so far and that would be enough, that Ella would feel cleansed without ever having to go that final, awful last step. More and more it seemed Angelina was right. But then she thought of Charlotte, the tiny, beautiful little angel, lying in her cot, coughing, red-faced, struggling to breathe . . . and eventually not breathing.

Still she couldn't do it.

She looked at Reuben again. In the distance the big man he'd just been talking to was heading into a small dark shack.

Reuben lifted a huge sack.

Last chance.

Then across the yard she saw someone walking towards her. A man in a coat wiping his hands on a red cloth, a look of puzzlement on his face as he came towards her.

So she turned, and forced her jellied legs to move back the way she had come, leaving Reuben behind.

There was always Monday.

Monday at noon.

★ ★ ★

One-Eyed George said, 'There was a fellow in here, earlier.'

Caleb Stone said, 'I'm glad. You wouldn't sell much whiskey if there wasn't.'

'He had one of those photograph things. Was showing it around asking if anyone had seen the fellow that was in the photograph.'

Cal felt a tightness in his neck as if someone had put their hands on his shoulders and was squeezing, but not in a nice way, not in the way that a woman could do it sometimes, but in a way that constricted the muscles all the way through your body, right through your chest, and all around your heart.

'It was his brother in the photo,' George said. 'The fellow you had Rudy shoot last Monday.'

Cal swallowed. It was still happening. More and more people seemed to be turning up, knowing his business, surrounding him. Closing in.

'Give me a whiskey,' he said.

George poured the whiskey. There were other men in the Engineer, a low level of conversation filled the place, the wind outside rattled the roof, and the stove emitted an intermittent hiss, like a snake sending out a warning.

'He knew his brother was dead,' George said. 'Knew that Rudy had done it, too.'

Cal downed the whiskey in one. He snapped the glass back on to the counter.

'Another please, George.'

'He'd been talking to Jack Byron, too.'

Cal drank half of the second whiskey. He sighed.

'I didn't tell him nothing,' George said.

'Who was he again?'

'Like I said, he's the brother of the man you had killed. His name is John Cavendish.'

24

Sam Loude paused his horse on the slight rise above Vista Quarry. The landscape was white as far as he could see. Every dip and crack and rabbit hole, and every place a horse could break a leg, was covered in snow. The trail up hadn't been so bad, and there was no snow falling today yet. Didn't look like there'd be any for an hour or two, either. Hell, overhead the sky was as clear and as blue as it was in summer. Sam took that to be a sign. He wasn't sure from whom. Maybe God. Maybe God was on his side. Yeah, maybe that was it. God didn't want hundreds of American boys being blasted to hell by Indians with Gatling guns. So God had eased up on the snow and let him and the horse see, for the most part, where they were headed.

But the quarry, itself set in a dip in the ground, a dip where the wind had blown the snow into great drifts, a dip in which many men had dug many holes, was a different matter.

Looking down at the quarry was like looking at a still white lake.

And there, on the far side of the lake, rising up out of the whiteness, were the few abandoned huts, one of which held frozen dynamite, which according to Rye Brewer you only had to look at and it would blow up in your face. Thank goodness God was on his side.

★ ★ ★

It wasn't as bad as it looked, although it was still back-breaking work. The snow was the light, powdery kind, and it was easy enough to shovel out of the way. He left the horse up on the ridge where she was shovelling snow out of the way with her nose, looking for some grass, and he slowly but surely dug a path towards the old huts. It occurred to him that if anyone came up here now, or even afterwards, what he'd done was as clear as if he'd written it down. But hell, he wasn't doing anything wrong. He'd paid for the dynamite. It was all — what was the word? — *legitimate*.

It took a couple of hours. The sun, burning out of that clear blue sky but not giving out any heat, had moved way across the sky before he had made it across to the huts.

But he was there.

Someone had even scrawled 'Store' on the door of the left-hand hut in blue — now faded — paint. The paint had run a little, as if it had been done in a hurry. He placed the shovel up against the hut. He sighed, and wiped his hands on his trousers. Then he turned the latch on the hut door and pulled.

Carefully.

That's what Rye had said. Do everything carefully. No sudden movements. It was like the dynamite was a riled Sioux warrior or something. Maybe a drunk back in the Engineer who was having a bad day. Don't even make eye contact. Tippy-toe around them.

The door squealed, and it seemed

to Sam that the whole hut moved and vibrated as he pulled it open, years of swelling and shrinking, of damp and dry wood, tightening the fitting between frame and door.

He held his breath.

Nothing happened.

So he stepped inside.

It was dark. Even after he stood still for a minute letting his eyes adjust, it was still dark. He thought back to what Rye had said about the crate. Not just that it was in the back of the hut, but that the dynamite would leak, and whatever it was that leaked you shouldn't even look at it. He felt a little like that dynamite now, feeling himself leaking, sweat rolling down his back and his flanks, down through his hair. Was he going to have to do this by feel, by touch? Hell, was it worth it? Was it worth the ride out here? Was it worth all that digging? Was it worth all this risk?

The thing was, Cal had sold him on the idea of doing business with the Indians over the whiskey. The drunker they are, Cal had said, the less likely they are to fight. But somehow the money had taken over as the driving force. Whiskey had turned into rifles, and now rifles were turning into Gatling guns.

It had become something different to what had been sold to him.

It had become something deadly.

So, yes, it was worth it. No matter how hard and no matter the risk. The way Sam had it figured he could blow those guns up even before they made it to the yard. The trains always paused on that slight grade just before the yard, waiting for the all clear. It took at least five minutes, sometimes a lot longer, for the yard man to get the signal out to the engineer. Sam could swing up on to the wagon, right there, slip the blasting cap into the dynamite, light one of the fuses, and be out of there and gone.

No one would get hurt and he could deny all knowledge so long as Rye kept his mouth shut. Maybe he'd need to clear out? He would see how it went.

But yes, it was worth it.

So he shuffled further into the darkness of the hut, and the floorboards creaked and moved beneath his feet, and he held his breath with every step.

Eventually Sam's eyes did adjust to the dark, and though he couldn't see much, he could see enough. The crate was pressed up against the back wall of the hut. There was a lid on the crate, but it wasn't nailed down or anything. Hell. That would have been crazy — even Sam realized that now.

Rye had written '*Dynamite, Careful*' in chalk on the lid.

Sam reached out, his fingers trembling, and lifted that lid. Gently, oh so gently. The lid came away easily, not like the door of the hut, and he swivelled from the hips and placed the lid on the floor. He turned back to the crate and he could see the dynamite. One . . . two . . . eight sticks all standing vertically in the crate, held tightly by the sand and dry hay packed around them. Eight sticks, and just looking at them he shivered and saw the future in his mind's eye — him picking up one of the sticks, taking it home, thawing it out. Him swinging up on to the train, lighting a fuse, seeing the boxcar explode. Then the image jumped to a battlefield and there were soldiers running forwards, not falling, *not* being slaughtered, but running, advancing. Winning.

Sam Loudes touched the nearest stick of dynamite. It was cold. He'd thought it would have been sticky, but no, it was just cold. Maybe it was damp? It was hard to tell. Hard to tell, like if you got a cut when you were freezing you weren't always sure if it was hurting or not.

He held his breath and he gripped the dynamite.

Very slowly he pulled it upwards, out of the mixture of sand and hay, away from whatever might have leaked out over the years.

It came out easily, just like it was meant to be. Just like he had God on his side.

And yes, it was frozen, and hadn't Rye said that meant it was safe?

Like so many things in life, it turned

out that all the worrying had been unnecessary. You just had to trust in your plans.

25

John Cavendish was eating a plate of bread and beans and drinking whiskey in a saloon called The Nugget. The bread was dry and the beans were cold. The whiskey had been poured from a bottle that had no label, and it tasted, so far as John Cavendish could tell, exactly like the whiskey he had drunk earlier at the place called The Engineer where the one-eyed owner had warned him off. He wished Alek were here. Alek was probably sitting in his favourite armchair with Grace knitting in the chair opposite, and that lovely fire roaring between them. Alek knew his drink. Alek would've known if this was the same drink. Cavendish was pretty sure it was the same, anyway.

He pictured the bottle that the deputy, Jack Byron, had poured a drink from the day before. John wished he'd accepted a drink there, now. Maybe the bottles meant nothing. Here in The Nugget he could see plenty of labelled whiskey bottles behind the counter. Nevertheless, he was just figuring that he'd compliment the barman on the whiskey next time he went up to the bar for a refill, see if he could get the man talking, when Ella Scarr walked in.

Heads turned. Somebody whistled. Someone else called out a good-natured obscenity. Somebody told the fellow to shut up, and somebody else laughed. Even before she'd taken two steps a tall fellow asked Ella if she would like a drink, and a short fellow asked if she'd like anything else. There was more laughter.

Then Ella saw John Cavendish sitting at the table on his own, his stick resting against the wall, and she walked on over and sat down.

'It's not quite as sweet as the Gold Rush,' she said, smiling. The smile straightened a little as she looked around at the cowboys and the yard workers, the drunks and the gamblers, the store owners and the drifters, some of whom were still staring at her, some of whom were turning away, going back to their drinks and their conversations now that they realized she wasn't alone.

'It's probably not the place for a lady,' he said, looking into her eyes, smiling himself.

'No,' she said. 'But I have my gun in my pocket.'

'You haven't . . .'

'No. I thought about it, though.'

He put his fork down on the side of his plate. 'What brings you here? I mean, I'm glad . . . No, I'm delighted to see you. But, this place?'

'They were strange towards me at the Beaumonts'. They said you'd moved out.'

'Yes.'

'They were really unfriendly.'

'They stole Luke's money.'

'What?'

He explained what had happened.

'I went back to The Horizon,' he said. 'You were looking for me, then?'

'I was.'

'How did you know I was here? I mean, you haven't hit every saloon in town, have you?'

'You'll be impressed,' she said.

'I will?'

'I saw footsteps outside. In the snow. I didn't think it was going to snow today, but it's pretty heavy out there again.'

'I know. I walked in it much of the afternoon.'

'I saw.'

She smiled again and he hoped she didn't see the way it made his shoulder shudder involuntarily.

'Outside there are footsteps. Loads of them, and amongst all the footsteps there's a little round indentation. Your stick.'

'You spotted that?'

'I wasn't thinking about it. I was walking along pondering on . . . well, on nothing really . . . and then I saw it and I realized it was you.'

'I'm not the only man in town with a cane.'

'You're the only one fool enough to be

walking around in the snow.' She smiled. Again, the smile hit him like something physical.

'I walked past this place and there were no more stick marks. I turned round. Came in. And here you are.'

'Are you after my job?' he said, and smiled back at her. Then he reached out and held her hand. 'It's good to see you, Ella.'

★ ★ ★

Arkansas Joe stood in the doorway to The Engineer and looked inside. It wasn't that busy, never was later in the evening. The men used this place all day long in between shifts, or during breaks, but in the evening they'd wander home, or head across the tracks where you could find a place that was a bit brighter and a bit warmer, somewhere that did food, and maybe someplace where you might find a woman, or some music. Or both. But there was Cal, at the table in the corner, a bottle of his own whiskey in front of him, staring at the stove as if the grey dented ironwork might answer all of his questions.

Joe ran his fingers down his thin beard and he pressed his tongue into the gap between his teeth. Sometimes it was best not to bother Cal. It wasn't that he had a temper. Quite the opposite. It was when he was quiet and calm that he was most unpredictable.

Joe swallowed, and pulled his collar up against the cold, which was almost as bad inside The Engineer as it was outside, and stepped up to the bar.

'Give me a glass, George,' he said.

Then he stepped over to the corner and said to Cal, 'Mind if I join you, boss?'

Cal looked up. His eyes were rimmed with red from the alcohol, the oil fumes, and the coal smoke leaking from the stove.

'Ah,' he said. 'My good friend Joe from Arkansas. What brings you out on such a warm evening?'

Joe sat down.

'It might be nothing,' he said. 'But I'm worried about Sam.'

* * *

Ella suggested going to Angelina's where they could talk and eat something a little more appetizing than the plate of cold beans that John Cavendish had been toying with. It would be warm, too, and it wouldn't be full of rude and leering men who smelled of beer and whiskey, smoke and sweat. 'Plus,' she'd said. 'I think you and Angelina will like each other.'

John Cavendish did indeed like Angelina. He liked her because she was funny and sweet, welcoming and generous. He liked her because she sat there in the kitchen with her grey hair and warm cardigan, and it reminded him that he had a cardigan back in his suitcase that had been knitted for him by someone who was probably right now sitting in a similar situation and who cared for him. And that was what he liked most about Angelina — she clearly cared an awful lot for Ella.

'You're a detective?' Angelina said.

He smiled. It meant that Ella must

have been talking about him to Angelina.

'I was,' he said. 'Until this.' He tapped his stick on the floor.

'But your leg's getting better?' Angelina said.

'Yes. I'm certainly getting plenty of exercise.'

'Where have you been today?'

'I've experienced the Quarters today.'

'Did you discover anything?' Ella asked.

'I discovered that they don't like talking to strangers down there.'

'I could have saved you a day's walking,' Angelina said. 'If you'd have asked.'

He smiled at her. 'Sometimes they tell you more with their faces than they do with the words they don't say.'

Angelina smiled, nodded towards Ella, and said, 'This one's like that.'

Ella smiled and shook her head at Angelina as if to say *stop it*.

'What did their faces say?' Ella asked Cavendish.

'A fellow down in the yard who did speak to me said that Luke had been there. I showed him this.' He took Luke's photograph from his coat pocket and placed it on the kitchen table. He watched Ella's eyes as she picked up the photograph. She blinked a couple of times and smiled at a memory. Then she handed the picture to Angelina, who said how handsome Luke had been, and what a tragedy it all was.

'He'd been asking about work,' John Cavendish told them. 'But not the manual work that the fellow I was talking to was doing. Luke had alluded to some deal that he thought was going on. He alluded to the same thing in a letter to me.'

'It wasn't Reuben, was it?' Ella said, her face looking momentarily worried. 'That you were talking to?'

'The man's name was Ray,' John said.

Angelina must have seen the brief flash of worry in Ella's face too, for she said, 'Was Reuben down there today, my dear? You went down there, too, didn't you?'

Ella said, 'Yes. I did go down there,

and yes, he was there.' She looked at John and said, 'I'll tell you about Reuben in a minute. I think it might help. It's partly why I was looking for you. But you finish first.'

John looked at her. He suddenly wanted to hold her, to protect her, to tell her that she shouldn't be down there on her own, not now he'd seen the place, not now he'd wandered around the yard, and the bar down there, and the maze of shacks beyond.

'Go on,' she said, holding his gaze.

'Ray said that a week or so ago — must have been a day or so before he was killed — Luke went down there and went into a place called The Engineer. It's a little saloon, I guess you'd call it. Just a dark shack, really.'

'I've seen it,' Ella said. 'From a distance.'

'Ray said Luke went in. He got the impression Luke had gone to meet someone.'

John picked up the photograph of Luke and looked at it, remembering his brother, wondering what he had stumbled into, and why it had got him killed.

'You went in there, didn't you?' Ella said.

'Uh-huh. It's run by a one-eyed fellow called George. He recognized Luke. I saw it in his eye. But he denied all knowledge.' He could see something in Ella's eyes, too. Some knowledge. A connection, maybe?

'It was more than that, though. He warned me off. He denied knowledge and then warned me off. What do you make of that?'

'Monday,' Ella said. 'Something is happening on Monday.'

She told them about going down to the yard, about the gun in her pocket, and about how she stood just the other side of the boxcar to Reuben.

She looked at Angelina. 'I couldn't do it. I was right there. But I couldn't do it.'

'I know, my dear. I've always known.'

'Then another man came along. His name was Cal. Caleb, I think. That's what Reuben said.'

Caleb, John Cavendish thought. The name rang a bell. Who had mentioned Caleb to him?

Ella described the man, and what he'd said about there being a load coming in on Monday at noon, and some of it going to the fort and some going up to the station. 'There's a man called Flynn, up at this station. Wherever it is.'

Angelina shook her head.

'Means nothing to me,' John said.

'Then,' Ella said, 'the one called Caleb went into that saloon, that dark shack, you just mentioned.'

★ ★ ★

Caleb Stone stood up, his legs unsteady, his mind worse.

Was it past midnight yet, he wondered. If it was already Sunday, that meant he only had to hold out for one more day. Maybe *hold out* wasn't the right phrase. But it was close enough. Flynn was dead and Rudy was dead and that newcomer — Luke   Cavendish — was dead, and now Cavendish's brother was in town asking questions, walking around with a photograph, of all things. And Arkansas Joe was saying Sam was having doubts. Who was to say that there weren't others out there? Others who knew. Others who were just lining up to . . . to do what? He was being too sensitive, he knew that. But it was hard not to be. What about Westlake? Who was to say Westlake hadn't said the wrong thing to someone? He walked to the door, looked out over the yard. The sky was black. It was snowing again. Flames illuminated the cabin of a locomotive as someone opened a firebox door. A fire burned by the side of the tracks, just some old sleepers, probably. Maybe someone was keeping warm over there.

'You all right, Cal?' One-Eyed George said from behind him.

'Heading home, George,' he said.

In two days he really would be heading home. Somewhere south.

But first . . . tomorrow he would go and see Sam. Arkansas Joe had been vague. It was probably just nerves, with Sam, the same as he had. Hell, they all had nerves. Especially this time. It was the big guns.

Nevertheless, tomorrow he would go and see Sam and judge for himself. If the man was losing it, or if Cal thought that Sam might be about to betray them, then he'd shoot him. Simple as. He liked Sam, but he'd shoot him there and then, right in his cabin in the South-West Quadrant. By the time the body started to stink up he'd be long gone.

26

John Cavendish woke up thinking about Ella Scarr and brother Luke. He was thinking about the way Ella had held the photograph of Luke, the expression on her face as she had looked at his brother. Her smile, the softness of her eyes at that moment. Was he jealous? No, that wasn't it. No more than usual, anyway. He'd always been a little jealous of his brother, the way he treated life so lightly, the ease with which he faced everything. John himself was more serious. But then he was the older brother, wasn't he? That was the way of the world. So, it wasn't jealousy. It was more inquisitiveness. He was, after all, a detective. He liked Ella and he wanted to know a little more — a lot more — about her. And part of that was what she had thought of Luke. How they had got along. What they had done together.

On Angelina's doorstep last night,

when he was heading back out into the growing snowstorm to limp back to The Horizon he had asked her why else she was looking for him.

'You said the stuff about Reuben was *partly* why you wanted to see me,' he'd said.

She'd smiled. It was a different smile to the one she'd made when looking at the photograph. This was a smile that made him feel like he was twenty years old again. She'd smiled, reached out and held his hand, and had said, 'I just wanted to see you again.'

Then she'd kissed him lightly on the cheek.

★ ★ ★

Sam Loude sat close to the stove, holding a tin cup of coffee in his hand, and stared at the canvas bag on the wooden crate by the stove.

He'd placed the bag on the floor alongside the stove yesterday. But then he'd got to thinking about whatever it was that might leak out. There might be more of it as the dynamite thawed, so he'd lifted the bag and slit the bottom in a couple of places, and then he'd placed it on a small wooden crate that had once held bags of grain. The crate itself had gaps between the strips of wood. Anything that dripped through the bag would dribble through the crate and pool on the floor.

Sure enough, there was something there. A drip now and again. Every time he heard that tiny splosh of the liquid he jumped, figuring he was about to die. But after an hour or two he realized it was water, nothing else. The dynamite was thawing, that was all.

So he sat and he drank coffee and watched the dynamite.

* * *

It was lunchtime when Caleb Stone hammered on Sam's door.

'You in there, Sam?'

Stone's head still hurt from all

the whiskey he had put down at The Engineer the previous night, and he could still feel the pressure building from all the unknowns, all the suspicions.

'Cal,' he heard Sam say.

Stone didn't wait for Sam to open the door. He pushed open the creaking wood and stepped inside.

'Warm in here,' he said.

Sam was over by the stove, doing something down by the floor.

'Just stoking her up,' Sam said. He sounded worried. Although Cal knew it might be his own imagination putting something into Sam's voice that wasn't really there.

Stone undid his coat. 'You got a fever or something?'

'No. I don't know. I was so cold last night that I got up and fed her too much coal. Would you like a coffee, Cal?'

'Sure.'

Stone sat down on the end of the bed. It sank under his weight.

'What brings you here?' Sam asked.

There was definitely something in

Sam's voice, Stone thought. It sounded thin, a little breathless. Like he was scared.

'Big day tomorrow. I'm just seeing all my boys. Making sure everyone's ready.'

'I'm good, Cal.'

He handed Stone a cup of coffee.

'Glad to hear it. Not scared or anything?'

'It's nothing we've not done a dozen time before.'

'Bigger guns, this time.'

'What's that old saying? Might as well be hanged for a sheep as for a lamb.'

'Not sure I've heard that one.'

'Well, it means we'd hang for rifles or we'd hang —'

'You think we're going to hang?'

'No. We've got it going smoothly, Cal. You've got it going smoothly.'

Stone stared at Sam. He was fidgeting a little, rocking from heel to heel. But Sam always was full of nerves and energy that way. Stone looked around the single room, the bed, the chair and the mirror hanging from a nail on the wall. The water jug and the cups and a few clay pots of whatever over there on a shelf by the stove. Some knives hanging up. Sam's few clothes strewn over the chair, and some others hanging from screws high up on the walls. A canvas bag over there by the stove.

'So you're good?'

'I'm good.'

'You happy here?'

'Come again?'

'Here. Julesville. The Quarters. This place.'

'It ain't much,' Sam said.

'You could afford something better, the money we've made.'

'I guess I could.'

'You got any ambitions, my friend?'

'How do you mean?'

'To move on? To go somewhere warm? To get a nicer place? You're young. You never thought of settling down? You know, with a woman?'

'You sound like a father!'

'Like I said, I'm just looking out for my boys.'

There was a faint splosh, the sound of a drip. It was nothing, but somehow it cut through into Stone's consciousness.

'I don't know, Cal. Maybe. How about you?'

'About the same,' Stone said.

It was coming from that canvas bag. He could see a pool of water beneath it on the wooden floorboards.

'What's in the bag, Sam? Looks like you've got a leak.'

'Oh that...' Sam turned. 'It's just... It's just half a rabbit. For later. I bought it off Marsh earlier. He had it outside all night. It's frozen solid.'

'Hell he find a rabbit this weather?'

Sam shrugged.

'But you're OK?' Stone asked. 'With everything, I mean?'

'I'm fine, Cal. There's no need to worry.'

Cal drank some more coffee and the rabbit dripped again, as it thawed out.

★ ★ ★

'In here again?' the bartender at The Nugget said.

John Cavendish smiled. 'Just having something to warm me up. It's cold out there.'

'Real pretty, the woman you were in here with last night. If you don't mind me saying.'

The bartender was young, maybe only twenty — right at that age that Ella made John feel again. He had dark hair and was wearing a clean white shirt beneath a smart vest. The bar was quiet compared to the previous evening.

'Yes, she is,' Cavendish said. 'She certainly is.'

He sipped the whiskey the boy had poured him.

'You know,' he said. 'This is good stuff.'

'Glad you like it.'

The bottle was still on the counter between them.

'What is it? I see there's no label.'

'I don't know. I can do you something else if you like.

But we get through plenty of this, and unless somebody specifically wants something else, this is what we sell. Caleb Stone ships it in. On the train. When I say 'shipped in', I mean . . . There are no ships here, are there? How far away you reckon the nearest ship is? A thousand miles?'

John Cavendish muttered something about a thousand miles being about right, but his mind was thinking about the fellow named Caleb Stone. So Stone was supplying the unlabelled whiskey. Was that what Luke had been trying to buy into? It didn't seem like the sort of deal that would get a man killed. It probably wasn't even illegal.

'You ever heard of a man called Flynn?' John asked the bartender. 'Works at a station — probably not the station here in town.'

The kid shook his head.

'Not aware of any other stations,' he said.

'Never mind,' John said. 'Thanks anyway.'

* * *

William Wainlodes's door was locked. John Cavendish, warm from the walk up town through all the snow, cupped his hand against the window and peered inside. The room was as empty and as tidy and as when he had first been there all those days ago.

He turned to go, and he saw Wainlodes walking towards him, smiling. Wainlodes and about thirty other people, all streaming out of the church, looking happy with life the way believers did after a good sermon.

'John,' Wainlodes said, holding out a gloved hand as he neared Cavendish. 'It's good to see you. Are you looking for me?'

'William. Good service?'

'Uplifting. Father Edwards mentioned your brother. We said a prayer for him.'

John Cavendish resisted the urge to ask if they'd said a prayer for Rudy Oliver, too.

'Tell him I said thank you.'

'I will.'

Wainlodes produced a key from his coat pocket. 'Come on inside. You did say you were after me?'

★ ★ ★

That evening John Cavendish knocked on Angelina's door, and like a young man outside a young lady's house, he waited.

Ella opened the door, her face beaming.

'John, you shouldn't wait out in the cold. Just come in.'

He stamped his feet, the left one as lightly as ever, and he brushed snow from his shoulders. He stepped into Angelina's tiny hall and he was close enough to Ella to smell her perfume, see the moisture on her lips, pick out individual eyelashes.

He wanted to hug her, but Angelina appeared at the end of the short corridor smiling herself, 'Is it him?' she said, as if they'd been talking about him again.

'I'm not sure who 'him' is,' he said,

holding Ella's gaze. 'But it's me.'

'Come in, my dear,' Gina said. 'I have a chicken cooking.'

He followed Ella into the kitchen, took his coat off, placed his stick against the wall and sat down. A cup and a teapot, milk and sugar, and a plate of biscuits appeared as if by magic on the table.

'Whilst we wait for the chicken,' Angelina said. 'So, what have you been up to today? We're dying to hear.'

'Let him have a drink first,' Ella said.

'It's OK,' John said, but he did reach out and pour milk and tea into a cup. He did the same for Ella just like he had on the day they'd first met. He poured one for Angelina, too, and she remarked on his manners and threw a quick smile at Ella.

'Caleb,' John said. 'The man you heard talking to your husband.'

'Husband,' Angelina said, as if the word tasted like rotten food in her mouth.

'Reuben,' Ella said. 'I can't think of him as my husband.'

'I'm sorry,' John said. 'The man you

heard talking to Reuben.'

'Yes,' Ella said. 'Caleb.'

'His surname is Stone. Caleb Stone.'

'You've found out about him?'

'He was the man who shot Rudy Oliver.'

'And Rudy Oliver shot Luke,' Ella said.

'Yep.'

'What does it mean?' Angelina asked, sipping tea.

'I'm not sure. Caleb Stone led the posse. I tracked down a fellow who was part of that posse. He said they wanted to bring Rudy in alive. He was a churchgoer, this fellow, and though there were a lot of emotions running high, the general feeling was they'd bring Rudy in and give him a fair trial. He told me that Caleb went ahead of them all — despite the posse's protestations — and shot Rudy dead. Caleb Stone insisted that Rudy drew on him, but this fellow said it made no sense. One fellow in the posse — I never met him — but his view, according to the one I was talking to, was that Rudy and Caleb had been friends. That they were into something together.'

'Maybe Caleb shot Rudy so that he couldn't tell anyone why he'd shot Luke,' Ella said.

'Who knows? But yes, I thought the same.'

'And this something that they — Rudy and Caleb — were into together. Maybe that's what your brother was trying to get into?'

'He was trying to get into something, that's for sure. Caleb Stone supplies whiskey to all sorts of people throughout the town. He supplies it to George, the fellow with one eye down at The Engineer — that rough old drinking hole in the yard. He supplies it to The Nugget — where you found me last night. I remember the sheriff — sorry, the deputy — drinking from a bottle. He, Jack Byron, knew that Caleb Stone had shot Rudy Oliver, too. Didn't seem bothered about it.'

'I never liked the sheriff, and I don't like the deputy,' Angelina said. 'Not that I know — knew — either of them.

Sometimes you can just tell.'

'Then there's the fellow called Flynn,' John Cavendish said, glancing at Ella, enjoying the way she looked impressed with him.

'Flynn?'

'You said yesterday that he was up at a station somewhere. That part of whatever load is coming in tomorrow is going up to Flynn.'

'Oh, yes.'

'Well I went to see William Wainlodes — you know, the undertaker?'

Ella nodded. Angelina said, 'He's a lovely man.'

'I went to see him because he struck me as a man who knows people. It was William who put me in touch with Quincy — that's the fellow who was in the posse. They go to church together.'

'You said the Pinkertons let you go?' Angelina said, smiling.

'Uh-huh.'

'They must be crazy.' Again she glanced at Ella.

'Who knows? When my leg is better

perhaps they'll think again?'

'I would certainly hope so.'

'Anyway, William Wainlodes told me the only Flynn he knew of was the Indian agent. Said he lived way up there. Way up where? I asked him. At the old relay station, Wainlodes told me.'

'The station,' Ella said.

'They like their whiskey,' Angelina said, 'the Indians.'

'But is it enough to get Luke killed?' John asked, looking from Angelina to Ella. 'I mean, it's not illegal selling whiskey to saloons, or even giving the deputy a bottle. Might not be legal to sell it to the Indians. But is that enough to get people killed?'

'I wouldn't have thought so,' Ella said.

'Me neither,' John said. 'I think we're missing something.'

'So what are you going to do?' Angelina asked.

'I'm going to ask Caleb Stone.'

'You know where he is?' Ella said.

John Cavendish said, 'I know where he'll be tomorrow at noon.'

27

By eleven forty-five on Monday the wind had picked up and the snow swirled in the air, seemingly rising as much as it fell. The blown snow drifted high against the siding buffers, the platforms, and the stationary wagons in the railroad yard. Men with shovels had cleared the tracks that the noon train was due in on, throwing the snow on top of the already high drifts. There was a sharper coldness in the air than previous days, and the chimneys of Julesville pushed out clouds of wood and coal smoke.

South of the railroad yard Sam Loude sheltered behind a tree and looked along the track, narrowing his eyes against the wind and the snow. It was like staring into a foggy day. His hands were clammy and his heart was beating so loudly in his chest that he was sure he could hear it just as much as he could feel it. He checked again that he had the Lucifers in his pocket.

'Come on,' he said to the train. 'Where are you?'

Then he saw her. One moment nothing, and then there she was, coming out of the blizzard, white smoke from her funnel almost invisible in the sky. A few seconds later the great grey and black locomotive was level with him, steam billowing from her pistons, her brakes squealing as she slowed, the smell of fire rising from her like sweat from a scared man.

He slid around the back of the tree as she slowed so the engineer and driver wouldn't see him. There was one last shriek from the brakes, and then she was still, the locomotive ahead of him now, already obscured in the snowstorm.

He peered at the far end of the train. There was an orange light burning within the caboose. But the window through which he saw the light was frosted. He knew the man — or men — in the caboose could look out at any time. But he had no choice. He had to do what he'd come to do.

He stepped out from behind the tree and, crouching low, ran towards the final boxcar. At the wagon he paused for breath, his back against the door. He couldn't see the caboose window light from here. That was good. But he had no time to spare. The signal could change at any time.

He reached up and yanked down on the handle of the boxcar, and slid the door open. He heaved himself up and in, pulled the door to, but left it open enough that a little light came in. There was just enough space in the wagon for him to crouch there, balancing between the freight and the open door.

The boxcar was filled with crates and boxes, sacks and bags. There were several large wheels with iron banded rims. There was writing on some of the boxes, but they were stacked in such a way that he couldn't make out the words.

He took a deep breath.

OK, it didn't matter which crates were which. He had eight sticks of dynamite.

The whole shipment would be blown to kingdom come. He told himself: *just do it and get out of there.*

From up ahead he heard the engine whistle blow.

Already?

He held out his free hand for balance and swung the canvas bag from his shoulder. Two days of sitting with the dynamite had seen his nervousness in its presence leak away, just like whatever it was that seeped out of the explosives.

He opened the bag, took out the sticks two at a time and pushed them in the gap between two long crates that themselves were balanced on two more similar crates. As he did so he saw the letters GAT stencilled on the edge of one of the crates.

God, he decided, was still on his side.

He took a length of safety fuse from the bag. It was already crimped on to a blasting cap. He gently pushed the blasting cap amongst the sticks of dynamite.

The train jerked and started to move.

'Easy,' he said. 'Easy.' He felt a trickle

of sweat run down his face.

He stretched out the safety fuse.

The train whistle blew once more.

He fumbled in his pocket for the Lucifers. His fingers were shaking and the train jerked again and the box of matches leapt from his hand as if it was alive. He looked in horror as the box fell to the ground and bounced off one of the crates. In that split second he had a vision of Cal unloading the guns, all of them intact, and discovering the dynamite and the fuse, of Cal turning to him, and...The matches came to a halt by his left foot, still inside the wagon.

He felt the motion of the train now, felt it pulling him forward to a destiny just a few hundred yards distant.

He reached down, rocking on his heels for balance, and grabbed the matches. He slid open the box and took a match out, flicked it against the rough edge of the box. It didn't light. He tried it again. The match broke.

The train was picking up speed now. It wasn't far. Just another minute, maybe less, and it would be braking, slowing to a stop in the yard.

He took another match.

This one flared into life perfectly.

He leant down, holding on to the door edge, and he applied the flame to the end of the safety fuse.

There was a moment when nothing happened. A moment long enough for him to wonder if the fuse was faulty, damp maybe, long enough for the vision of Cal finding the dynamite to appear again. But then there was a fizzing sound as the fuse caught, a small flame burst into life, and tiny sparks jumped into the air around the fuse.

Sam Loude stood up and eased himself out into the freezing day. He slid the door as far shut as he could whilst still giving himself something to hold on to, then he leapt backwards into the snow.

★ ★ ★

'Where are the others?' African Joe said. He looked at Caleb Stone. 'Sam and Arkansas?'

Caleb was thinking the same thing. The train was in. It had slowed to a halt right in front of them. A guard had jumped down from the caboose, said good morning, and was already heading up to the locomotive, banging his gloved hands together. Reuben Scarr had backed up a two-horse wagon in front of the boxcar. African Joe had driven another one down, a one-horse wagon, which he'd positioned in front of Reuben's.

'They hitching the other wagons, Rube?' Stone asked.

'Nope. They're all ready, over by the sheds. Just waiting for someone to bring 'em down. No idea where your boys are.'

It wasn't right. Caleb could feel it in his bones. They'd always been here on time, every other occasion when there hadn't been anything at stake. Then, this time, when for days he'd been feeling that unease, that pressure in the back of his skull, they weren't here.

'You want we should start unloading, Cal?' African Joe said.

Then, from between the boxcar and the caboose, stepping over the couplings, Sam appeared. He had his hands in the air and behind him was Arkansas Joe, his rifle pointing at the middle of Sam's back.

'I don't know what's going on,' Arkansas Joe said, looking at Caleb Stone. 'But he was making a run for it. Got his horse back there. All his bags, and everything.'

★ ★ ★

John Cavendish heard their voices moments before he saw the men. He was picking his way through the snowdrifts piled up against a row of wagons that looked like they hadn't moved in months, heading towards the train that had just pulled in. Smoke hung over the locomotive, steam hissed from somewhere. He made it to the rear of a broken wagon that was resting at such an angle he wondered if it hadn't actually rolled off the end of a siding, and stopped.

A fellow he'd never seen before was standing alongside the train that had just pulled in — he was in front of the last wagon, his hands in the air. He kept trying to move away from the wagon, but another fellow had his rifle levelled at him.

'I can explain!' the man said, stepping forwards.

'Stand still, Sam, for Chris'sakes,' a big man said. His beard had grey in it, his shoulders were wide. There was an element of command in his voice. He was wearing a mountain-man fur coat. It was the man Ella had described the previous night. Caleb Stone.

'I wasn't running away, I swear,' the one called Sam said.

'Then what were you doing?'

Again Sam tried to step away from the wagon, and again the man with the rifle poked him backwards, until he was standing against the wagon.

Along from the boxcar John Cavendish saw another man sitting on the bench of a flat-bed cart, twisting around, watching the proceedings. There was a fifth man, too. Dark skinned. He was standing by Caleb Stone, shaking his head as if he couldn't believe what was happening.

'I thought I saw someone out there,' Sam said. 'I don't know. Army, or someone.'

'You thought you saw someone?' the man with the gun said. 'That's why your horse is back there loaded up with your bags?'

'Sam?' Caleb Stone said. 'What have you got to say?'

* * *

Ella Scarr knew that John wouldn't have let her anywhere near the railway yard at noon on that Monday. Not that he had any say in what she did, of course. But she didn't want to ask, be refused, and show up there anyway. It was better not to ask, and simply turn up.

She wasn't sure why she needed to be there. It was a little to do with Reuben, to see what he was really up to, and it was a little to do with Luke. After all, he'd died because of this. But it was mostly to do with John. She liked John. She *liked* him a lot. He had something that his brother hadn't — oh, Luke had the charm and the boyish looks and the carefree roaming attitude, but where did all that get a woman? No, there was something about John that was deeper, and maybe a little sadder. She supposed some people would have preferred the carefree brother. But wasn't that the way of the world? Different people liked different things. When your husband had lit out with another woman, then carefree roaming mightn't be what attracted you.

But it wasn't John's seriousness or depth that had brought her here. He was still injured, still weak from that terrible injury he'd suffered back east in the summer. He was resourceful and intelligent, and, it seemed to her, fearless. But this Caleb Stone was a killer. He probably wouldn't think twice about shooting John. But maybe if there was someone else there, too. And if that someone had a gun, too. Well, who knows, it might help?

She'd headed down to the yard and had seen John from a distance. He was edging along that line of abandoned wagons. The snow had drifted high up against their sides and she could see how he was struggling to walk through it.

She didn't want John to see her. Not yet. Maybe not at all. So she crossed the lines up by the station building and worked her way down on the far side of the noon train, rushing, stumbling a little, trying to get down there before John showed himself. Wanting to be in place in case he needed help.

★ ★ ★

'Sam?' Caleb Stone said.

'I told you he was up to something,' Arkansas Joe said.

The snow was swirling in Caleb's eyes, hundreds, maybe thousands of individual flakes, and there were just as many random thoughts being blown around inside his head too. He'd known it was going bad. He should have paid more attention to his feelings.

Sam moved again, and this time Arkansas Joe hit him hard in the stomach with the barrel of his rifle. Sam screamed, and doubled over, and as the scream died a woman gasped.

'What the hell?' Caleb said.

African Joe said, 'What was that?'

'Other side of the wagons,' Caleb said.

'I can see her,' Reuben said, standing up on his wagon. The he said, 'My God. Ella!'

★ ★ ★

John Cavendish saw it all unfold. The dark-skinned man went one side of the boxcar, and the fellow who'd been in the wagon — Reuben, John guessed, by the way he'd exclaimed Ella's name — went the other.

It was the dark-skinned man who caught her, pulling her back this side of the boxcar with an arm around her throat and a gun in his hand. He let her go and she stood there glaring at Caleb Stone.

Reuben came back between the wagons.

'Who the hell is this?' Caleb Stone asked.

'What the hell's she doing here?' Reuben said, his face turning dark. 'That's my . . . wife.'

★ ★ ★

It was the way he said it. Condescension and irritation in his voice. As if she was nothing, maybe an inconvenience at best. It was the anger and fury in his face. It was as if he couldn't believe she had the wherewithal, the guts — even the right — to look for him, to track him down. He came towards her, his hands like claws and his lips drawn back over his teeth, and there was hate, real hate, in his expression. Right then, she was knew he was nothing but evil. Not a person. Not skin and bone. Just a cheating bag of evil.

'You killed our baby,' she said, and from her pocket she pulled out that gun that he'd bought her all that time ago, back when she'd believed in him, back when Charlotte was still alive.

★ ★ ★

John Cavendish stepped out from his hiding place.

'Ella! Don't!' he cried.

She didn't even look at him. She was raising the gun and staring at Reuben and he was reaching out for her and John Cavendish could see her finger tightening on the trigger.

Then the dark-skinned man hit her arm so hard with his own gun that Ella dropped the tiny gun she was holding and screamed with pain.

Reuben was on her then, hands around her throat, and the dark-skinned man hit him, too, and he fell to his knees.

Caleb Stone looked at John Cavendish and said, 'Who the hell are you?'

'My name is John Cavendish,' he said. 'And you killed my brother for this...' John pointed to the boxcar '...whatever's inside it.'

Caleb Stone opened his mouth to say something, but right then came the sound. It was a sizzle, like a pork chop being dropped on to a hot skillet. It lasted just long enough to register as a mystery, and then came a bang, as sharp as a rifle shot but a hundred times louder, loud enough to hurt the ears. There was another bang, and another, so close that they might not have existed at all. Then a flash and the smell of burning, followed by a roar as if an entire lightning storm had been cooped up inside the boxcar and had suddenly burst free. The doors flew off, not sliding open, but scything through the air like broken windmill sails. The roof lifted. Pieces of wood and metal blew out of the ruined boxcar. A wheel spun through the air, and John Cavendish felt himself lifted up, as if a great hand had simply reached down, grabbed him, and flung him backwards.

He hit something hard, although he was aware that a great depth of snow had softened the blow. The snow enveloped him. Something pierced his leg. He wanted to scream but there was snow in his mouth. He heard more explosions, and it even sounded like there was gunfire within the explosions. He shook his face to clear the snow and he could see smoke and fire pouring from the boxcar. The roof, or a chunk of it, that had been blown upwards came crashing down, and John Cavendish watched in horror as it hit Reuben, crushing his head like a rotten melon. Someone was moaning. He could hear Ella crying. Hear distant shouting.

Then Caleb Stone was rising up in front of him, unmarked, standing there like a bear, a gun in his hand, rage on his face.

* * *

'You had to get involved, didn't you?' Caleb Stone said. His ears were ringing from the blast and he couldn't hear his own words, wasn't sure how loud they were coming out.

Sam was dead. Arkansas Joe was dead, too.

Caleb had seen it happen. Right there in front of his eyes. Sam had just . . . disappeared. It was as if he'd never existed. He'd taken the full force of the blast and was just gone. And Joe next to him. Caleb shook his head. He didn't want to recall what he'd just seen happen to Joe.

He had his gun in his hand. Didn't recall drawing it. But it was there and it was already pointing at this John Cavendish lying there buried in the snow, just his face and shoulders showing. Cavendish was still alive, but already blood was staining the snow around where his legs would be. Well hell, Cavendish wasn't going to have to worry about that for long.

'What did you do?' he said.

It must have been what Sam had seen. He'd surely spotted something and had been trying to tell them. Those bags on his horse... Arkansas must have been mistaken. Sam had been OK.

John Cavendish shook his head. Maybe he said something, Caleb wasn't sure. His ears felt full of cloth. There were more explosions, more noise, behind him.

'Your brother should've taken no for an answer,' Caleb said.

He could feel the pressure in his head. It had been there all week, but now it was really pushing on his ears. He could feel it at the back of his eyes. He wiped a hand against his nose and it came away covered in blood. He could taste blood, too. That pressure was forcing the blood out of him.

Something occurred to him.

'You fight in the war?' he said. There was blood coming from Cavendish's nose, too. The snow covering Cavendish's legs was scarlet. He didn't want the man to die. He wanted to kill him. He *needed* to kill him. Needed to relieve that pressure.

'Did you?' he said. 'Tell me!'

Cavendish looked up at him, fear in his eyes. That was good. That was nice.

Cavendish nodded.

'Who?' Stone said.

Cavendish said, '183rd Pennsylvania.'

The words cut through Stone's muffled ears.

'I knew it,' he said. 'I knew you were a Yankee.'

He thrust his gun forwards and squeezed the trigger.

★ ★ ★

Ella tried to stand. She could smell burning, and for a moment she thought her hair was on fire. She slapped at her head but there were no flames. Her arms hurt, both of them. Her head spun. She managed to get to her knees as if she was praying. There was blood in her mouth. She became aware that lying in the snow next to her was the dark-skinned man who had grabbed her on the other side of the wagon. She was suddenly scared, fearing he was about to grab her again.

But then she saw a piece of metal embedded in his throat. He wasn't breathing.

She took a deep breath. Blinked several times. The snow was still falling, as if all that fire and noise hadn't affected it at all.

Now she saw Caleb Stone — who else could it be? He was standing amongst all of the wreckage, all the fire and smoke, the blackened debris spread around his feet and he had a gun in his hand and he was pointing it at...

She saw John then — he was lying up against one of the old wagons, blood on his face, almost totally buried in the snow, and that snow...There was so much blood around his legs that it looked like he was lying beneath a crimson blanket.

'I knew you were a Yankee,' Caleb Stone said, and she saw the gleam of delight in his eyes, saw him lick his lips. She heard men yelling, knew they were coming closer, and she urged them to be faster.

But they were too far away and she saw Stone's finger squeezing the trigger, caressing it, savouring the moment.

* * *

It had been the Seventh Street cut all over again. The storm of metal and wood and fire, the noise and the smoke, the smell of fire and the gunshots. It was as if he was still there, as if nothing that had happened between then and now was real. It had all been a dream and the battle with the strike-breakers was still happening. He could feel the pain in his hand where something had hit him, but it was nothing compared to the pain in his leg. He hadn't seen what it was, but he knew it was bad.

Then, for a moment, he thought he was in a hospital bed again. It was white and soft, although colder than he remembered. But now a shadow rose up before him, a devil, untouched by all the carnage, seemingly impervious to it. And the devil looked down upon him, and he realized he was still in the middle of a battle. Except it wasn't the cut: it was the Julesville railyard. He felt something solid against his shoulders, maybe a wheel. He realized it was snow, not blankets, enveloping him.

He shook his head to clear the snow from his face, and it was Caleb Stone standing before him, his eyes dark, blood pouring from his nose and mouth. Caleb Stone who had as good as killed Luke.

Caleb Stone was talking to him. John Cavendish couldn't make out the words. He shook his head again.

'You fight in the war?' Stone said. At least, that's what John thought he said. There was snow pressed into his ears, too.

Then Stone said something else: he was asking who John had fought with.

'183rd Pennsylvania,' John said. If he'd had the strength he'd have said how damn proud he was of it, too.

Then Caleb was grinning like a demon, raising that gun, calling John a Yankee — and John looked into Caleb's eyes, and from beneath that deep blanket of snow he pulled the trigger on his own gun. Once, twice, three times, seeing the surprise on Caleb Stone's face.

Blowing him backwards to hell.

Epilogue

In Reading, Pennsylvania, Alek Nowakowski was reading the newspaper, a glass on the table next to him. Grace sat opposite. She was knitting. It was the first time in months that they hadn't lit a fire. It had been a long winter, and many times they'd thought they'd never be warm again.

Alek lifted his glass and admired the amber liquid. It was French brandy. The finest French brandy.

'Who do you think it was?' he said.

She smiled.

'It was John,' she said.

'But why?'

'Because he could,' she said. 'Somehow he could.'

'Where do you think he is?'

'I don't know.'

She looked at the wool in her hands. It was beautiful English wool. The wool and the brandy — scores of balls of wool, and a dozen bottles of brandy — had arrived in well packed wooden cases the week before. There had been no card, no return address.

'He knows we wouldn't have taken money,' she said.

'You think he found the easy money he went looking for?'

'I don't think there's such a thing as easy money.'

'But he found something?'

'I think so.'

★ ★ ★

William Wainlodes said, 'It's time. Do you need both sticks?'

John Cavendish said, 'No, just one will do.'

'You sure?'

'Uh-huh. When the moment comes I want to be able to hold her hand.'

William smiled.

William Wainlodes stood up and with just the slightest pressure on John's elbow he helped John up too.

They both looked straight ahead, but

then there was the slightest change in the air, a breeze almost imperceptible as a door opened. They heard a few whispers and someone saying, 'She's so beautiful' and neither John nor William could contain themselves. They both looked round and here came Angelina, and on her arm, Ella Scarr, looking radiant in a long white dress, smiling and trying not to cry, as she walked up the short aisle of the Julesville church. John Cavendish found he had tears in his eyes, too.

She drew level with him, smiled, and looked into his eyes. She mouthed *I love you* and he told her he loved her, too.

Father Edwards coughed and they both laughed and managed to break their gaze. They turned and faced the priest. He smiled, too, and whispered 'Are you both OK?'

'Yes,' Ella said.

'John?' Father Edwards asked. 'All good?'

In his pocket John Cavendish could feel the photograph of Luke. He never did get to see Luke again, and he missed his brother so much it hurt. The money had been hard money, too, for both of them. But he glanced over at Ella and knew that it had all been worth it. He knew that Luke would have been happy, too. In fact, knowing Luke the way he did, he'd bet his brother would have said he'd planned it all just this way. Luke always did want him to be happy.

'Yes,' John said, and stole another look at Ella. 'All is very good.'

We do hope that you have enjoyed reading this large print book.

Did you know that all of our titles are available for purchase?

We publish a wide range of high quality large print books including:
**Romances, Mysteries, Classics
General Fiction
Non Fiction and Westerns**

Special interest titles available in large print are:
**The Little Oxford Dictionary
Music Book, Song Book
Hymn Book, Service Book**

Also available from us courtesy of Oxford University Press:
**Young Readers' Dictionary
(large print edition)
Young Readers' Thesaurus
(large print edition)**

For further information or a free brochure, please contact us at:
**Ulverscroft Large Print Books Ltd.,
The Green, Bradgate Road, Anstey,
Leicester, LE7 7FU, England.
Tel:** (00 44) **0116 236 4325
Fax:** (00 44) **0116 234 0205**

*Other titles in the
Linford Western Library:*

HOGAN'S BLUFF

Harriet Cade

When his father is killed and his sister kidnapped following a confrontation with a powerful rancher, it falls to fourteen-year-old Zachariah Hogan to set matters straight. That this would entail his riding with a band of Sioux warriors was something that the boy could not, in his wildest dreams, ever have imagined. So it is that a youngster who has not even yet begun to shave becomes embroiled in the last action of the Great Sioux War of 1876 . . .

DESERT JUSTICE

Paul S. Powers

Sonny Tabor is a man charged with a string of murders, feared for his accuracy with a gun, and relentlessly pursued by those seeking the reward being offered for his capture. But he is also a man wrongfully accused, shooting only in self-defence, and forced into a life of perpetual flight. From being captured and sentenced to hang, to being abandoned in the desert handcuffed to an Arizona Ranger — will he ever clear his name and find the true guilty party?

BODIE

James Hitt

Lawyer Josh Thorn believes in law and justice. Even so, when he agrees to defend prostitute Rosa May Whitefield, he knows he jeopardizes his standing in the community. The California mining town of Bodie averages a killing a day, but Rosa May's crime broke all the rules when she shot one man dead and wounded two others because they had beaten and raped her. Powerful forces line up against lawyer and client, and Rosa May's fate appears sealed — can Josh save her?